Cameron
Comes Through

Cameron *Comes Through*

Philip McCutchan

St. Martin's Press
New York

For information, address St. Martin's Press, 175 Fifth Avenue, New York, N.Y. 10010.

Library of Congress Cataloging in Publication Data

McCutchan, Philip, 1920-
 Cameron comes through.

 1. World War, 1939-1945—Fiction. I. Title
PR6063.A167C26   1986   823'.914   85-30406
 ISBN 0-312-11444-3

First published in Great Britain by Arthur Barker Limited.

First U.S. Edition

10 9 8 7 6 5 4 3 2 1

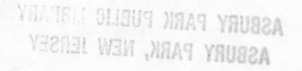

Cameron
Comes Through

1

MALTA in May 1941, when Cameron arrived to join *Wharfedale*, was an island fortress under siege and under almost constant attack from the air. There was bomb damage everywhere: Cameron's first impression on arrival had been of heaps of sandstone, shattered and lying as junk around the steep, stepped streets of Valletta and Senglea. The whole place seemed filled with the British Navy, at least in the evenings when the bars and brothels of Strada Stretta, known to generations of seamen as The Gut, did their usual brisk trade. Indeed bars were everywhere, mostly named after ships past and present of the Mediterranean Fleet upon which the people of Malta depended almost entirely for their living: the Queen Elizabeth Bar, the Resolution Bar, the Revenge Bar and very many others. It was all something of an eye-opener for Donald Cameron: it was a far cry from his home in Aberdeen, not least weather-wise. In May Malta began to swelter, and the Fleet, or such of it as lay in the Grand Harbour, or French Creek, or Dockyard Creek, or in the Coastal Forces base in Sliema Creek, shifted into Number 13s, in other words white shirts – or 'flannels' in the case of the lower-deck seamen and stokers – and white shorts, with white cap covers to lighten the winter blue of home waters.

It was a change, too, from the rigid formality of HMS *King Alfred*, whence Cameron had gone after leaving the old *Carmarthen* in Rosyth and being put before the Admiralty Selection Board at the Royal Naval Barracks, Portsmouth. On acceptance for training for a commission as sub-lieutenant,

5

RNVR, he had gone with some seventy other CW candidates to the first part of his three-months' course, held at Lancing College in Sussex. The surroundings were idyllic to an ordinary seaman fresh from the fo'c'sle messdeck of a destroyer pitching and rolling to the North Atlantic gales and suffering the attacks of U-boats and the German long-range Focke-Wulfs. Nevertheless, Ps and Qs had to be minded at all times, for the cadet ratings, as they were now called, were under close scrutiny of the *King Alfred*'s executive and instructor officers from start to end of each day. Behaviour in the bar, deportment, meal-time manners – these things counted, if perhaps not quite so much as gunnery, torpedoes, navigation, seamanship, signalling and parade-ground drill. Officers were still expected to act as gentlemen. The cloistered ambience of Lancing helped; the unfinished municipal swimming baths at Hove, which housed Part Two of the cadet ratings' course, helped less. The cadet divisions were accommodated in what was intended to be, and but for the outbreak of war would have been, an underground car park; and the garage-like, concrete surroundings were a good deal less salubrious than the Lancing dormitories. Nevertheless, at the end of the second six-week period Donald Cameron, Cadet Rating ex Ordinary Seaman, passed the examinations, went before the final Admiralty Board composed of elderly admirals and captains and emerged on to the dignified streets of Hove as Sub-Lieutenant Donald Cameron, Royal Naval Volunteer Reserve, proud possessor of a single wavy stripe on either cuff, a stripe that in pre-war days would have been of pure gold thread but under the exigencies of war had become a yellowish substitute known as Orris lace; and, moreover, in the interest of economy, went only half-way round the cuff instead of right round.

'Never mind, gentlemen,' the course Gunner's Mate said, addressing them as such for the first time next morning. 'Half-way doesn't wear out the pockets like all round does – or so they tell me.'

It was satisfactory enough, in any case. It had been worked

for and won. From now, life would be totally different, though the dangers to be faced would be no less than before. At the passing-out board, each new officer had been asked by the President in which branch of the service he would like, if he was given the chance, to serve; Cameron had answered, 'Destroyers, sir.'

'Why?'

Cameron said, 'I liked the *Carmarthen*, sir.'

'In what way?'

'A good ship's company, sir. And I know something of what it's like now, sir.'

The Admiral had given him an approving look. 'Well, I suppose that's as good an answer as any. And you still want to go back?'

Cameron nodded. 'Yes, I do, sir.'

'Well, perhaps you will, though it's in the hands of NA2SL,' the Admiral said, referring to the officer holding the appointment of Naval Assistant to the Second Sea Lord, whose department in the Admiralty, housed in Queen Anne's Mansions off Birdcage Walk, dealt with all officer postings to the Fleet and shore establishments at home and abroad. 'I'll add my recommend for what it's worth – and good luck, my boy.'

'Thank you, sir.'

Cameron had a further fortnight to spend at the Hove swimming baths to complete training, this time as an officer, learning an officer's divisional and other duties: learning his responsibility towards the men of his division, the men with whose day-to-day lives he would become involved, not always as the giver of orders but often as friend, corrector and adviser on personal problems brought to him via his divisional petty officer. The relationship would not always be an easy one and would depend largely on his own personality and character, especially when dealing with men many years his senior in age and naval experience. The fortnight passed quickly; in the evenings, Cameron, exchanging for a white starched collar and black tie the white roll-neck sweater that was the rig, beneath the monkey-jacket, for officers under training at *King Alfred*, went ashore to enjoy such night life as was to be found in wartime Brighton. There was more freedom now: no more tiered bunks in the subterranean car park, but lodgings in Hove under the aegis of a youngish widow who soon began giving her lodger many inviting looks. These he failed to respond to; Mary Anstey, now a Leading Wren, was still somewhere in his thoughts. Mary had had a fortnight's leave during his time at *King Alfred*, and she had come down from home for an evening to see him, a little self-consciously, wondering, he believed, if she was being too obvious. He had put her at her ease and given her an expensive dinner at the Norfolk Hotel. He believed that his request to be sent back to destroyers could have had something to do with Mary's presence in Rosyth; he might be appointed to one of the escorts operating, as *Carmarthen* had done, from Scottish waters.

But in the event he wasn't. He was at home on leave when his appointment came through from Queen Anne's Mansions: his orders directed him to report two days' hence at 1500 hours to the Navy Office in Albert Harbour, Greenock, for passage overseas to join the destroyer *Wharfedale* as replacement for a sub-lieutenant killed in action. He went down from Aberdeen next day to see Mary in Rosyth, and the following day reported as ordered to Albert Harbour, which was full of drifters, many of them brought down from Stornoway with their own peacetime crews of fishermen to act as tenders and liberty-boats for the warships anchored off the Tail o' the Bank or shackled to the buoys. He was informed by a trim Wren that he was to take passage to the Mediterranean in the battle-cruiser *Repulse*, lying at the flagship buoy and due to sail for Gibraltar at 1800 hours.

Out into the Firth of Clyde through the boom, leaving Cloch Point to port, *Repulse* steamed with her great turreted fifteen-inch guns, behind the destroyer escort, down towards Toward Point at the entrance to Rothesay Bay where the old depot-ship *Cyclops* acted as parent to the Seventh Submarine Flotilla. On past the Cumbraes to leave the Isle of Arran to starboard as she made down towards Ailsa Craig, standing seagull-whitened beneath a potentially brilliant sunset. Out above Northern Ireland and the Londonderry escort base, into the Atlantic, making some westering in order to drop down on Gibraltar in a wide arc well clear of the coast of occupied France and unfriendlily neutral north-west Spain. They entered Gibraltar some seven days later. In the inner harbour Cameron recognized *Repulse*'s sister-ship *Renown*, wearing the flag of Vice-Admiral Sir James Somerville, commanding Force H which with *Renown* included the aircraft-carrier *Ark Royal* and the heavy cruiser *Sheffield* with their destroyer escorts. Signals were exchanged between *Repulse* and the Tower in the dockyard: among more pressing matters it was indicated that a message would arrive by hand of officer within the next half-hour indicating the onward destination of Sub-Lieutenant Cameron. Two hours after this, he found himself transferred with his gear to HMS *Foresight*, a destroyer of the Force H escort. Aboard *Foresight* he was told that *Wharfedale* was in Malta.

That night, under cover of the darkness and with no time allowed for shore visiting, the destroyer slipped out of Gibraltar, bound through the Mediterranean with an important supply and ammunition convoy that included some troop-ships for Alexandria; *Foresight* was under orders to detach for Malta with ships carrying vital food and oil fuel for the island, while the other ships of Force H steamed on with the main body of the convoy.

Cameron had been buttonholed for action duty by the First Lieutenant immediately he had set foot aboard *Foresight*. 'No room for passengers in a destroyer,' Number One said.

'I know, sir.'

'You do, do you?' Lieutenant Parsons looked him up and down. 'Been in destroyers before?'

'I was in *Carmarthen*, sir, doing my sea time.' Cameron added, 'North Atlantic convoys out of Scapa, sir.'

'Yes, I know, and don't keep calling me sir – other than on duty in front of ratings, that is. Number One'll do the rest of the time.' Parsons frowned. 'I heard the story – who bloody well hasn't – of a rating who chucked grenades down a U-boat hatch and blew the bugger up. A cw rating – wasn't it?'

Cameron grinned. 'Yes.'

'You?'

'Yes, it was.'

Parsons blew out his cheeks. 'Bloody murderer . . . I don't mean that really. What a fantastic show, though! Must have been like putting ferrets down a rabbit-hole.'

'I rather hope I don't have to do it again,' Cameron said. 'I've always had a certain sympathy for things caught in traps . . . like rabbits with ferrets after them.'

'I take your point, old chap. Anyway, you won't find any U-boats in the Med – they'll be swarming here one day I don't doubt, but so far they haven't come through the straits. The Eyetie submarines are a rather softer option – but what we have to worry about is the Gap!'

'Gap?'

'A gap in the deep minefield laid across the Narrows between Sicily and Pantellaria, where the water's just too deep to be mined. That's what we have to get through to reach Malta, and that's where the buggers concentrate their dive-bombers – while we're in irons, as it were. We go through the Gap at night, of course, but it doesn't make a hell of a lot of difference – the sods always find us out. You'll see! You'll see because at action stations I want you in the conning-tower as a spare Officer of the Watch if anyone buys it on the bridge. All right?'

They were ghostly beneath a bright, unkind moon that brought up the big ships' massive silhouettes: the great fighting-tops of the *Renown* standing out above her main armament; the enormous and ungainly bulk of the *Ark Royal*; the smaller, leaner outline of the *Sheffield*; and the sturdy

10

hulls of the ships in convoy – the former Orient Liner *Orontes*, a stately ship with two funnels and two masts, carrying an infantry brigade to the Middle East; the Canadian Pacific Line's *Empress of Britain* similarly loaded and bound, two fast tankers to supply Malta's air and military needs, two ammunition ships for Alexandria, and two food ships for Malta's relief. Malta was said to be down to eating rats and mice; taking convoys through the Gap was a business that had all too often ended in glorious failure. Ahead and on the wings steamed the destroyer escort; aboard *Ark Royal* the old Stringbags, the Swordfish torpedo-bombers, were ready to be ranged on the flight deck when needed by the Admiral. In case of Italian fleet movements – the battleships *Vittorio Veneto* and *Giulio Cesare* were believed to be at sea with their destroyers – heavy units of the main Mediterranean Fleet under Admiral Sir Andrew Cunningham would be on station to the south of Sardinia. As the convoy moved eastwards each ship was starkly illuminated by the sea's phosphorescence as the bows clove through at something approaching twenty knots, phosphorescence that lit the bones in their teeth and streamed back along the sides in green light that added to the ghostly effect of the night.

Dusk action stations had been piped as soon as the warships of the escort were off Europa Point, where they had reduced revs to allow overtaking by the convoy, which was moving through the strait to meet them from the west after dropping their escort from home waters. Cameron was at his allotted station in the conning-tower when the Captain's voice came down.

'Cox'n?'

The Torpedo-Coxswain answered, 'Cox'n here, sir.'

'Something wrong with the bloody tannoy. I want to speak to the ship's company. Send an electrician up.'

'Aye, aye, sir.' A messenger was despatched at the double. The ships steamed on. Cameron stepped outside to take a look at the moving, blacked-out vessels. He was feeling awkward; in his brand-new uniform he looked brand-new himself

11

– and was, of course; the men in the conning-tower would know, or easily guess, that in his last ship he had been an ordinary seaman, lowest of the low, and had been elevated over their experienced heads. There might be resentment, probably would be from some of them at least, and more importantly the same would apply to the *Wharfedale* when he joined her in Malta. That could make life difficult; and, oddly perhaps, it was something he hadn't thought about until now, when they could be moving into action and he would be expected to react as an officer if things went wrong. Initiative would be called for, that most officer-like of all the OLQ factors.

Apart from the engine sounds and the low hum of the ventilators there was a curious silence, a night silence, until the repaired tannoy came up loud and clear, bringing the Captain's voice to all parts of the ship.

'This is the Captain speaking. There's been a signal from Gibraltar – the main Italian battle fleet is reported on station westward of the Gap. Admiral Somerville is taking the heavy ships ahead to engage, in support of Admiral Cunningham's battleships and cruisers, while the destroyers remain as the close escort for the convoy. The ship's company will remain closed up at first degree of readiness until further notice. That's all.' The clipped tones ceased, and the tannoy clicked off.

Cameron felt a curious sensation in his stomach: convoy escort was one thing; surface action against the immense gun power of the Italian battleships and cruisers was quite another. Back in the conning-tower he met the eye of the Torpedo-Coxswain, faintly outlined in the soft glow from the gyro repeater before the wheel. He said, 'Sounds ominous, Cox'n.'

'Not a bit of it, sir. We've had these scares before now. Know what happens, sir?'

'What?'

'The Eyeties see our big ships ... and they bugger off. You mark my words, sir. They've got the speed and they use it. It's

12

at once the whine of the incoming enemy aircraft was heard. They came in with the afternoon sun behind them, zooming high over the island to release their bomb-loads. The bombs were seen, dropping in clusters like eggs.

'Your welcome to Malta, Cameron,' the Captain said.

said they mount their biggest guns aft, 'cos they're always bloody retreating!'

In the event, this proved to be the case. The heavy ships of Force H, gone from the convoy's vicinity by the time the dawn came up, were reported by the lookouts towards noon, returning to rejoin. As they came up and turned to take station, the signal was made, general from the Flag by masthead light: ENEMY DISPERSED AFTER INITIAL EXCHANGE OF GUNFIRE. NO CASUALTIES OR DAMAGE. That was all; the rest was left to the imagination: Admiral Somerville's ships would not have had the speed to catch the Italian fleet even if he had felt it wise, which for a certainty he would not, to jeopardize the vital convoy by detaching the main strength of the escort for long enough to be of use against the Italians; any chase could be left to Admiral Cunningham's Mediterranean Fleet units. For similar reasons he would not have flown off his torpedo-bomber strike force of Swordfish from *Ark Royal*; the carrier was needed to rejoin the convoy and use her aircraft to attack any surface vessels that might appear over the horizon.

And the convoy was not to be left unmolested: that night, still beneath a bright moon, the ships entered the Gap. Away to the south lay the rocky island of Pantellaria, to the north lay Sicily with its squadrons of dive-bombers and torpedo-bombers; to both north and south the deep minefield stretched. The aerial attacks began soon after the convoy was in the minefield. Down they came, diving through the bursting shrapnel from the ack-ack batteries, screaming in to aim their bomb-loads and their torpedoes. The sky was full of noise and menace. Cameron was called to the compass platform when the Officer of the Watch, a shoulder badly torn by shrapnel, was taken below to the sick bay: just as Cameron reached the compass platform, he saw three aircraft come down in the water not far off. Shortly after this one of the ammunition-ships went up, shattered to fragments by her own exploding cargo as she was taken by a tin fish from a torpedo-bomber that had gone screaming into her starboard beam at little more than a foot above the water before lifting to skim the decks. The whole sea seemed to be lit up with an immensity of flame that dimmed the moon, and the shock waves thudded through the destroyer like blows from a sledgehammer. It was obvious that there could be no survivors, unless some of the bridge personnel had by some miracle merely been blown clear. In any case, this was the sort of situation where survivors could not be picked up. Shortly after the ammunition-ship had gone, there was another explosion away to port and fire lit the fo'c'sle of one of the laden tankers. The fire appeared to be confined to the fore end but would surely spread aft whatever the efforts made to control it.

Suddenly there was a shout from the Captain. 'See that, Cameron? Fine on the port bow!'

Cameron looked, and saw: an enemy aircraft, shot down, was still afloat; the pilot was climbing out along the wing and could clearly be seen, waving an arm towards one of the escort, whose course was a little to port of him. As Cameron watched, the destroyer's bows came round, just a little.

Cameron asked, 'Do you pick up ditched pilots, sir?'

'Like hell we do! Just you watch.'

Cameron watched. The pilot was waving still – perhaps, like Cameron, expecting rescue before his plane sank under him. But the fast-moving, knifing bows, aimed dead on target now, cut through both plane and pilot like a bacon-slicer.

'Bugger asked for it,' the Captain said with much satisfaction.

The attacks went on through the night; there were no more sinkings although hits had been scored on two of the troop-ships and there had been a number of casualties. A little before dawn the attackers withdrew towards Sicily and no more came out. Both convoy and escort took stock of themselves: by now the stricken tanker had burned out and was gone, sunk beneath a spreading, flaming patch of oil fuel. The survivors of the convoy steamed on; the damage to the troop-ships was not enough, their masters reported, to need assistance. One of the escorting destroyers had been sunk and

another was sufficiently damaged for'ard to have to fall out from the escort and be taken in tow of one of her sister-ships.

The rest proceeded at maximum convoy speed towards Malta and Alexandria. As they began the approach to the besieged island, the detaching orders came from the Flag and the Convoy Commodore: the food ships and the remaining tanker for Malta were to break off in company with HMS *Foresight* and enter the Grand Harbour.

It had been quite a successful convoy. Malta was appreciative of it. By invitation of *Foresight*'s captain, Cameron was on the compass platform as the ships came slowly in through the breakwater and on past Fort St Angelo into the Grand Harbour. From every vantage point – from Fort St Angelo itself, from Custom House Steps, from Senglea, from the warships in the port – hands waved and cheering came. The sun was bright, and shone down on an outwardly happy island. But the happiness was no more than skin deep and was but temporary in any case. Everyone was on the point of starvation and there had been much damage, and not only to the island itself. From the water not far inside the breakwater, masts and funnel-tops pierced the blue water of the harbour, mute evidence of the bombs and magnetic mines that were dropped often enough inside the harbour entrance from enemy aircraft, to seal in the ships and prevent entry of supplies.

The Captain had been this way before. Grimly he indicated one of the sunken wrecks, that of a destroyer. 'She went two months ago,' he said. 'They haven't got all the bodies out yet.' As *Foresight* came farther in, he drew Cameron's attention to another destroyer lying in Dockyard Creek off the Grand Harbour. 'There you are,' he said. 'Your ship, Cameron. I wish you luck aboard her. They're a good crowd – her Captain's a good friend of mine.' He grinned. 'I don't suppose you've many illusions left about life out here being all sun, swimming and gin sessions – have you?'

Cameron was about to answer very positively that he hadn't when from ashore there came the sound of the air raid sirens. Immediately, *Foresight* was sent to action stations; and almost

2

'WE'RE delighted to have you, I can tell you,' *Wharfedale*'s First Lieutenant said, and obviously meant it. 'Being short of a watchkeeper's not been too easy. You've not had any experience yet, but you'll learn fast! We don't do an awful lot of harbour time these days – it's far too damn dangerous!'

'I can well believe it,' Cameron said. The raid hadn't lasted long, but the explosions indicated a good deal of damage ashore, while in Dockyard Creek, astern of *Wharfedale*, a bomb had hit the jetty and had flung sandstone and fragments of metal far and wide; *Wharfedale*'s decks had been dirtied but that was all – they'd just been dead lucky. Cameron asked, 'How long before I'm allowed to take a watch on my own?'

The First Lieutenant, who had introduced himself as Michael Drummond, shrugged and lit a cigarette. As an afterthought he passed the packet to Cameron, who took one. Drummond said, 'At twenty for sixpence it's hardly an expensive habit, is it? To answer your question, old man – it's up to you. Shine, and Father will approve you.' Father was the name customarily accorded a Captain by the wardroom. 'You want to aim to get your watchkeeping certificate as soon as possible, then you're all set to take charge of a watch at sea in your own right – but you know that, I dare say. Now you'd better come along and be introduced to Father.'

Father – Lieutenant-Commander Rodney Sawbridge, RN – proved to be a cheery-faced man with a loud and infectious

17

laugh, short and square in build and with big, freckled hands covered in ginger hairs like his head. He, too, was delighted to have his officer complement restored. Also, like the First Lieutenant of *Foresight*, he had heard about that U-boat in the North Atlantic.

'Hand-grenades, my word!' he said. 'Never heard such impudence. Adolf will never recover from the shocking indignity. What's your other experience, briefly summarized?'

'*Royal Arthur*, sir, then *Ganges*. And Commodore's Guard at RNB Portsmouth. After that, *Carmarthen* and *King Alfred*.'

'H'm. Well, you have a lot to learn yet – and you'll learn it if you value your life. We're all interdependent – make a balls and you'll kill yourself along with the rest of us, Cameron. As it happens, we're stuck here in Malta for two more days – an engine-room defect. That gives you time to familiarize yourself with the ship, its equipment and potential, and the men. Make the most of it.'

'I will, sir.'

'Right, good, then that's all for now,' Sawbridge said briskly, and rubbed his big hands together. Drummond took the hint and gestured Cameron to leave the Captain's cabin. As Cameron reached the door, he was called back. 'Make the most of Malta once shore leave's piped,' Sawbridge said. 'There used to be a saying, pre-war ... all work and no play makes Jack a dull boy. I believe in that saying. Right?'

Cameron returned the smile that had accompanied the words. 'Right, sir,' he said.

That evening, he took the Captain at his word. He went across the Grand Harbour to Valletta with the other sub-lieutenant, an RNR named Hugh Bradley, who had suggested a run ashore during tea in the wardroom, a brief meal of a cup of strong tea with sandwiches of somewhat vague origin, followed by fruit cake. Most of the officers had been present; apart from the Captain and the First Lieutenant, the officer complement consisted of two other lieutenants – both RNVR – two sub-lieutenants and a midshipman, the latter taking on, in

18

addition to his upper-deck duties, the task of Captain's secretary, since destroyers carried no paymasters. The non-executive branches were represented by the Surgeon-Lieutenant, who was RNVR, and the Warrant Engineer, who was RN. Additional to the executive officers was the Torpedo-Gunner, also a warrant officer RN. During this, his first real experience of shipboard wardroom life, Cameron was somewhat nervous and reserved but was quickly put at his ease by his new brother officers. It was all very different from the *Carmarthen* and Able-Seaman Tomkins. It was much more comfortable, too; and Cameron, who was to share a cabin with Hugh Bradley, appreciated the semi-privacy of that.

Bradley proposed taking him to a bar unofficially used by officers only. 'Doesn't do,' Bradley said, 'to drink with ratings. Men are apt to get drunk, and when they do, awkward scenes can occur. That's to be avoided. Do you know why?'

'Fights?'

'Fights, exactly,' Bradley said, 'but not just the fact of getting involved in a fight. The point's this: officers never put themselves in the position where a rating might have to be charged with striking them – get it?'

'I think so,' Cameron answered. He was constantly returning salutes as he walked along; Malta was all Navy. 'We always have a care for their own protection?'

'That's about it.'

They had not yet reached the bar when the next air attack came in and once more the sirens wailed. Within seconds, as it seemed, the streets were clear of Maltese and only British servicemen were seen – Navy, Army, RAF. Malta was a garrison, all of it, served by the Maltese more or less in the capacity of camp followers. The attack was a fairly heavy one, and the crumps of the falling bombs indicated a lot more damage. But the sky was soon filled with the bursts from the ack-ack, both ship and shore based; and after this the Hurricane fighters went in, climbing, weaving, diving. Malta was Mussolini's *bête noir*, the unsinkable aircraft-carrier that gave him nightmares.

He was doing his best via his allies to destroy Malta's morale. But he wasn't going to succeed. The RAF would see to that.

Cameron and Bradley got to the bar somewhat the worse for wear: a bomb, exploding at the end of the street they were in when the attack came, had thrown them flat and their white uniforms were covered with dust and in places torn. They had their drinks and a meal once the All Clear had sounded and the bar staff had come back to duty. They met some girls, English girls working at the Under Twenty-One Club in Valletta; then they returned aboard from Custom House Steps, taking a *dghaisa* across the Grand Harbour's moonlit water. The warships looked stark, forbidding, silhouetted as they were against the silvered sandstone behind, the rising, clustered alleys of Senglea beyond the Naval Victualling Yard.

They returned to a degree of panic.

'Captain wants you as soon as you come aboard, sir,' the quartermaster on duty at the gangway said to Bradley. 'And you, sir,' he added to Cameron.

Bradley nodded. 'Thank you, Gaunt. What's in the air, d'you know?'

'No, sir, not really, sir. An officer come aboard half an hour ago with a hand message.' Able-Seaman Gaunt paused, weightily: it was nice to have officers hanging on his words for once, instead of the other way round. 'There's a buzz, sir, that's all.'

'Oh, come on, Gaunt, what's the buzz about?'

'Crete, sir.'

'Crete!'

'That's right, sir. There's, what, around twelve thousand brown jobs in Crete, according to the buzz, like.'

'Uh-huh. What else does the buzz say, Gaunt?'

'Nothing else, sir. Nothing else at all. Maybe it's all wrong anyway, sir.' Gaunt looked innocent. There might well be nothing in it, but in Gaunt's experience, a long experience testified to by his three good conduct badges, buzzes emanating from the galley wireless more often than not held at least a grain of fact. While Gaunt cogitated on buzzes, the two officers made for the Captain's cabin; in there, all might be revealed and Gaunt's information by-passed. In the meantime there was always something about unsubstantiated buzzes on board any warship whose ahead movements were for ever uncertain. It was a kind of masochism; you always hoped that somehow or other a home leave might come into the next movement order, but of course you knew very well it never did.

It didn't this time; far from it. And the Gaunt-borne buzz, if incomplete, was by no means inaccurate.

'Glad you're back,' Sawbridge said, standing by his wash-hand cabinet while his officers sat around him wherever a rump could find purchase. 'Something's come up and the moment we're ready for sea – as I've been telling the Chief – we'll be under orders to move out. This time, it's not a convoy.' He paused, running a hand through the thick ginger hair. 'I'm ordered to join the Med Fleet units that are trying to stop any enemy seaborne landings in Crete and trying to keep the sea lanes open for supplying our garrison there. It's not going to be a picnic, I need hardly tell you.' Sawbridge went on to sketch in the background: when Greece had fallen, and large numbers of Allied troops had been taken by the Germans, a decision had been made to hold Crete, to which many troops had been evacuated from Greece. Now the German High Command had determined to take the island for themselves and already there had been attacks by bombers, with parachute landings backed up by gliders and transport planes. Admiral Cunningham had made his dispositions, and when the attack had started three days earlier Force A – the battleships *Warspite* and *Valiant* with their destroyer escort – had been steaming about a hundred miles west of Crete to cover the light forces; subsequently the cruisers *Gloucester* and *Fiji* with more destroyers had been ordered out from Alexandria to join Force A, which was also to be reinforced from the Antikithera Strait by the cruisers *Ajax*, *Orion* and *Dido*. The aircraft-carrier *Formidable* was standing by in Alexandria with her fighters and bombers; the

21

battleships *Queen Elizabeth* and *Barham* were ready also. Sawbridge went on, 'I'm ordered to leave Malta the soonest possible, and join the Fifth Destroyer Flotilla which has already gone to sea. Any questions, gentlemen?'

'Yes,' the First Lieutenant said. 'We seem to be committing a hell of a lot of ships, sir. Big stuff and all . . . it almost looks as though they're going to be required for an evacuation, doesn't it?'

Sawbridge nodded. 'It's in the air. Nothing definite yet, but for my money that's the way it's going to go. Which is where we come in, as a matter of fact.'

'We're not just going to redress the balance, then?'

'One poor bloody destroyer wouldn't redress many balances, Number One. If anything, we'd be a drag on Lord Louis's flotilla . . . he has the speed that we haven't. No, we've been given a special mission, and it remains with me alone, by personal order of the Vice-Admiral, until we've cleared away to sea. Then I shall tell the whole ship's company. In the meantime, all I've said tonight is to be regarded as Most Secret classification. Understood?'

There was a murmur of assent. Sawbridge said, 'See to the general readiness, Number One. Stores, ammunition, the lot. And there'll be no more leave piped till we get back. Chief?'

The Warrant Engineer looked up. 'Sir?'

'Speed's of the essence, Chief. Do your level best to get ready for sea, all right?'

'All right, sir.'

Sawbridge nodded and pushed himself off the bulkhead. 'That's all, then. Those that can, get some sleep. There won't be much more of it.' As the officers left the cabin, Sawbridge called Cameron back. He said, 'You're being thrown in at the deep end, Cameron. First ship as an officer . . . it's going to test you out. How d'you feel about it?'

'Scared, sir!'

Sawbridge laughed and clapped him on the shoulder. 'I'll bet you do! So do I. It's not a bad feeling to have. It's the best way of being kept on your toes. And I've no doubt at all you'll cope.'

There was a greater fear to drive Cameron on, and that was the fear of showing fear. Officers above all must not be seen to be afraid; that way, the rot set in and in any case there was the question of pride. His chief doubt concerned his actual abilities to take charge of a situation, if he had to, in an emergency. True, he had to some extent done so in *Carmarthen*, but there had been a vital difference: as a rating, he had not been *expected* to take charge; now, he would have to do all that was required of an officer and if he couldn't his name would be mud.

He was realizing his inexperience fast. There was as yet all to learn. Before he had gone ashore that evening, Number One had outlined what his various duties would be. He had been allocated to the FX or fo'c'sle division as assistant to the Divisional Officer – Roberts, one of the RNVR lieutenants, whom he would also understudy as assistant Cable Officer responsible for anchors and cables and the bringing of the ship to a buoy or to anchor, and for the handling of the fore ropes and wires when coming alongside. His cruising station would be as second Officer of the Watch until he had been pronounced fit to take a watch of his own. In action his station, for the time being, was also to be second Officer of the Watch, a position in which he would be readily available to the Captain should he be required to take over from any officer killed or wounded. He was forced to recognize that he was being regarded as something of a spare hand; this was bad for the ego but was perfectly understandable. Green officers if unsupervised could kill men.

That night he was kept busy until the early hours; the First Lieutenant took the opportunity of acquainting him with stores lists and how a ship was prepared for sea in all manner of unromantic ways involving much paper-work. That, and the more practical aspects of overhauling the deck gear and the guns and torpedoes and firing circuits, much of which was the responsibility of the Torpedo-Gunner, or Gunner (T) for short, one Mr Vibart, Warrant Officer. Mr Vibart lost no time in telling Cameron, whilst instructing him in the intricacies of torpedo circuits, that he had been in the Navy for thirty years.

'A long time, Mr Vibart.'

'A very long time, yes.' Vibart gave a sniff and wiped his nose on the back of his hand. 'An' all I got out of it's a thin stripe, not like some. Still, that's the way of the world, I reckon.'

Cameron said nothing to that; he recognized that Mr Vibart didn't go much on RNVR sub-lieutenants and he couldn't blame him. The Gunner (T) went on morosely, 'We're in for it this time. Special missions ... they're always 'orrible. Ends in bloody murder every time.' He stopped work for a moment and stared round the Grand Harbour, at the moonlight on the water and on the close-set buildings. 'Best say hail and farewell to bloody Malta while you can. I don't reckon we'll ever see it again.'

Cameron tried to be cheerful and produced a cliché. 'Never say die, Mr Vibart.'

'Die, eh?' The Gunner (T) stopped work again and glared. 'Don't use that word, Mr Cameron, *please*. I reckon we're all marked men in the bloody Med ... know what they call the Med out here, do you?'

'No?'

'Cunningham's pond,' Mr Vibart said dourly. 'We're all his little fish ... and once in, we don't get out again, not till we're bloody dead we don't. They say he stops every draft out of the Med with his own bloody pen. Greedy for all the 'ands he can get hold of.'

The Warrant Engineer worked miracles, as was expected of him. By 0730 hours he reported his engines ready to turn over for trial, with steam on the boilers for immediate notice. The engine trials proved successful, and Sawbridge ordered his First Lieutenant to pipe special sea dutymen. Climbing to the compass platform he authorized the signal to the Castile, the

24

shore signal station, reporting readiness and asking formal permission of the Admiral to proceed to sea in execution of previous orders. As soon as that permission came via the King's Harbour Master, the orders were passed.

'Let go headrope and sternrope . . . let go spring . . . engines slow astern.' As *Wharfedale*'s stem came round and off the wall, the after spring was let go and the engines put ahead. When all ropes and wires had been brought inboard the hands fell in fore and aft for leaving harbour. The early-morning scene was one of peace and beauty; the sun shone down on the bright blue water that contrasted so strongly with the old yellow-white buildings as the destroyer moved through the Grand Harbour, her bosun's mates piping a salute to the Admiral as they headed out for the breakwater leaving Fort St Angelo to starboard. Cameron watched the receding harbour and hoped the Gunner (T)'s words had been just hot air. At 0815 *Wharfedale* passed the breakwater outwards and her engines were put to full ahead. She began her race to join Lord Louis Mountbatten and his Fifth Flotilla, and within minutes of clearing away from Malta Sawbridge spoke over the tannoy to his ship's company. Or started to; he had scarcely pressed the switch when a lookout reported:

'Aircraft coming in, sir, bearing red nine-oh.'

3

THE incoming aircraft were identified as German: early in the year the Luftwaffe had moved Flieger-korps x into Sicily's airfields. As the dive-bombers, accompanied by twin-engined fighters, roared in, the alarm rattlers sounded throughout the destroyer and Sawbridge rang down emergency full ahead on the engines. As *Wharfedale* surged on, Sawbridge started a zig-zag; and as he did so, the Hurricanes scrambled from the about-to-be-attacked island behind. They climbed high in an attempt to drop down on the dive-bombers, and the ack-ack defences put up their barrage. *Wharfedale*'s anti-aircraft fire joined in; the sky was dotted with white puffs as the shrapnel burst. The dive-bombers seemed to take no notice; down they came, screaming, and Malta erupted in numerous places. As two of the enemy aircraft peeled off towards *Wharfedale*, the close-range weapons stuttered into action, the pom-poms and Oerlikons pouring out their rounds. There was a stench of gun-smoke and the whole ship seemed to lift in the air as a near miss from one of the dive-bombers took her. Water dropped aboard, cascading over the compass platform.

'Bastards,' Sawbridge said flatly. 'No damn manners.' He spoke to Bradley, action Officer of the Watch. 'Hard-a-starboard, Sub. We've got to shake them off, like fleas.'

As the helm was put hard over, the destroyer heeled

sharply, her starboard side lifting as the port rails went almost under: the manoeuvre was only just in time. Another near miss shook the hull and more water dropped aboard. Then came something better, something that was due to sheer luck: one of the attackers failed to pull out of its dive in time and drove smack into the Mediterranean some two cables to port of the speeding ship. The wings broke off on impact, like matchwood; the aircraft's own impetus carried it down deep, and no more was seen of plane or crew. There was ragged cheering from *Wharfedale*'s upper deck, cheering that was renewed when two more enemy machines were shot up by the Hurricanes and plunged in flames. By now *Wharfedale* had as it were got her hand in; she was covering herself with an umbrella of anti-aircraft fire and, twisting and turning as she was, presented a difficult target. The dive-bombers broke off the attack.

Sawbridge wiped his face with a handkerchief.

'Malta's stationary,' he remarked to no one in particular. 'Easy enough to hit, poor sods. I can only wish them luck.' He shook a fist back towards the German attack force as it peeled off for the island, still harassed by the RAF Hurricanes. 'All right, Sub, stop the zig-zag. Get the shipwright to sound round and report. Cameron, go below with the shipwright – it's a good opportunity to acquire some knowledge of damage control among other things.'

'Aye, aye, sir,' Cameron said. While he was below, the tannoy clicked on for Sawbridge to pass the promised movement information to his ship's company. *Wharfedale*'s special mission seemed likely to be a tricky one: she was to lie off the south coast of Crete and put a party ashore between the ports of Sphakia and Tymbaki to bring off a person or persons as yet unknown.

Sawbridge said, 'The identity or identities are obviously known to the British Government, but I shall not be told until we're off the coast, when I shall be contacted. Once we have our man, or men – or women for all I know – aboard, then I'm under orders to join Lord Louis, after which we come under

27

his command. For the present, that's all I know.' He paused. 'I expect to be off the south coast of Crete by midnight tonight. The ship will be at action stations from 2000 hours – if not before.'

The tannoy clicked off.

There was, for the time being, no further enemy action; both sea and sky remained clear. It could have been a peacetime cruise if it hadn't been for their sustained high speed, speed that set everything rattling in the wardroom when Cameron went down for lunch.

He found the Gunner (т) there, sitting in an armchair and reading a days'-old copy of the *Times of Malta*. On Cameron's entry, Vibart threw the paper aside.

'Give me the *Mirror* every time,' he said. 'Roll on Pompey, eh!'

'I thought this was a Devonport ship, Torps.'

'So it is, but I'm not. I'm *Vernon*, right?' Vibart's reference was to HMS *Vernon*, the torpedo and anti-submarine school in Portsmouth. He blew out a long breath. 'I wonder what perisher's waiting for us in Crete. I don't like this. Hanging about off the coast, it's not my cup of tea. Give me the wide open hogwash, every time!'

'I suppose we may not be there long.' Cameron sat down. 'Whoever we have to pick up . . . they'll presumably be ready for us.'

'Unless the Germans get to them first,' Vibart pointed out. He scratched his chin. 'According to the buzzes, Crete's not a healthy place, Sub. Not healthy at all. All those troops brought out of Greece, and Hitler can't wait to knock 'em all off – well, stands to reason he'd want to, eh? Whole island under constant attack, you can bet your young life on it. Not that I'm scared,' he added. 'It's what I joined for, I suppose . . . but I've got a wife and four kids to support. Not much future for them on a WO's widow's pension! You youngsters, you just don't know how lucky you are. War's a single man's game if you ask me.'

Cameron nodded. The married men did indeed have the worst of it; they had more to lose, and he remembered that aboard *Carmarthen* it was the married men who had always had a preoccupied look about them and who were the most avid for the BBC News broadcasts and to get at the papers when they returned to port. The air raids were never far from their minds; even the evacuated children were far from safe in the so-called safe country areas; often enough the Luftwaffe jettisoned its bomb-loads on country districts and the nagging anxiety was always there. Yes, it was better to be single in a world at war, and never mind that so many men of his age seemed to be propelled by the fact of war itself into quick marriages, as though they wished to snatch at happiness before it was too late. That was a point of view, of course, but basically a selfish one. As for Cameron, he had a strong feeling that he was going to survive this war and the rest could wait. Nevertheless, the Gunner (T)'s words had made him uneasy: it was tricky, hanging about off a coast that by the sound of events as reported in rumour was becoming a happy hunting ground for the Third Reich. From what the Captain had said the night before, C-in-C Med was worried enough to commit most of his big Fleet units and that spoke for itself. Lunch over, it was back to the compass platform. The new sub-lieutenant might soon be required to replace a casualty, and before that happened he must become as familiar as possible with the handling of the ship at sea and learn to a hair's-breadth how much helm would be needed to alter course under various conditions of speed and weather.

With the sea and sky both remaining clear, the Captain went below and left the bridge to his navigating officer, Hugh Bradley, Sub-Lieutenant RNR. In peacetime Bradley had been doing an apprenticeship with the Clan Line and had obtained his Second Mate's certificate just before the outbreak of war. He had been many times through the Mediterranean and was reasonably well versed in bridge watchkeeping; though, as he said, a Clan liner handled very differently from a destroyer.

29

Cameron, he forecast, would soon get the feel of her, as he had done.

'Nothing in it,' he said off-handedly. 'A little trial and error and there you are.'

Cameron asked, 'Could I try an alteration of course, d'you think?'

'Not unless you want to incur Father's wrath. Wait till he's up here himself. Then he can say "no" in person.' Bradley grinned. 'He has an ETA to keep to, old man. Just watch and observe when we start some manoeuvring, which'll be after we're off the Crete coast tonight. That's something I don't look forward to particularly, I must admit ... we're going to be something of a sitting duck, waiting to embark this unknown VIP. It's going to be a rotten job, you know.'

The destroyer steamed on through a flat calm, throwing back a big bow-wave that curled up around her hawse-pipes and rushed aft to join the wake's turbulence. There was a subdued roar from the fast-turning engines and the whole ship seemed to be straining with a curious urgency, almost as though she felt in her plates that she was desperately needed by hard-pressed men in Crete.

Sawbridge returned to the compass platform after a brief sleep and sent Bradley below while Cameron was given the unexpected thrill of taking over the watch; sleep was important, for after 2000 hours no one was going to have the chance of any at all, and throughout the ship men were being sent below for a spell, then returning to relieve their mates on the guns and torpedo-tubes, the signal lamps and lookout posts, and in the engine-room and boiler-rooms. Sawbridge was taciturn, standing in the forepart of the compass platform and staring ahead, sometimes using his glasses to examine the horizon as his ship rushed onwards. After a while he swung round and spoke to Cameron.

He said, 'Don't get me wrong, old chap, but you'll realize I'm speaking nothing but the truth when I say that currently you're my least valuable officer. Any Captain would be bound to say that of his newest joined sub-lieutenant. Understand?'

'Yes, sir.'

'Good.' Sawbridge smiled and seemed relieved. 'That is, at sea. But you can be bloody useful ashore and do a job that has to be done as well as anyone else. In short, I'm sending you ashore tonight to make the rendezvous and bring off our man. All right?'

'Yes, sir,' Cameron said again, and felt a surge of excitement run through him. And sheer, naked fear at the same time, a feeling that he fought down firmly. It was on everyone's lips, it seemed, that Crete was no picnic and here he was, being projected right into the heart of it, well away from the ship which, however fragile she might be against bombs and guns and torpedoes, had a sight safer feeling about her than the still-distant shores of Crete...

'You won't go alone,' Sawbridge was going on. 'You'll have a petty officer, a leading-seaman and twelve men, including a signalman. You'll all be armed – you and your PO with revolvers, the leading hand and the junior ratings with rifles. Two hundred rounds of ammo per man, and bayonets. And something else.' He grinned. 'You may guess what.'

'Hand-grenades, sir?'

'Right! You'll get detailed orders just as soon as I get them myself. In the meantime, you'd better have a word with Number One and sort out who's to be detailed for your party – and after that, get to know them.' Sawbridge bent to the voice-pipe. 'Quartermaster?'

'Sir?'

'Send a messenger down to Lieutenant Renshaw. My compliments and I'd like him to take over the watch.'

'Aye, aye, sir.'

When Renshaw came up, Cameron went below and found the First Lieutenant. Drummond said that Petty Officer Pike, PO of the Fo'c'sle Division, would be a tower of strength;

31

so would Leading-Seaman Wellington. They would be detailed, and between them they would pick the right hands to form the party. When the party was detailed and mustered, Cameron had a word with each of them, finding out his service experience and then chatting with them all in a general way as a step towards gaining their confidence. He felt he was really being thrown in at the deep end now, with a vengeance. As an officer, it might make him and it might break him. Once ashore, all the decisions would be his alone and all lives would be in his hands, which was a daunting thought.

'Green as grass is subby,' Leading-Seaman Wellington said reflectively as he fished a dog-end out from inside his cap and lit it. He blew smoke past Petty Officer Pike's left ear. 'Roll on my bleeding twelve! Think we'll ever see Guz again?' he asked, using the lower-deck name for Devonport.

'Don't ask me,' Pike said. He was a small man, bright-eyed and wizened beyond his years, with brown flesh puckered around his eyes as though he had spent a lifetime gazing into long distances. 'Cameron'll be all right, I reckon. He looks like he can take it and come up smiling. Didn't do so bad in the *Carmarthen* according to the buzz, eh?'

Wellington didn't answer that; instead he gave a belch and said, 'Wonder who the geezer is who has to be picked up. I heard a buzz down The Gut that the King of Greece had done a bunk to Crete. Maybe he's the one.'

'Could be,' Pike said. 'We'll be told soon enough, anyway.' He went off to confer with the Gunner's Mate about issuing the revolvers and rifles for the landing-party, then he disappeared into the petty officers' mess to write a letter to his wife in Devonport, though God alone knew where and when it might be posted. If the ship bought it, it never would be. But the ship might survive while he did not; landing-parties could be bloody terrible and if any man had wanted to be a soldier, well, then he wouldn't have joined the Navy – stood to reason,

32

did that. Young Cameron didn't know what he was in for, but he would soon find out. And he, Pike, would make bloody sure the officer didn't go and do anything too daft. Petty Officer Pike wished very badly that he could tell his old woman where he was going so that maybe the blow would be softened if he didn't get back off Crete, but the wardroom officers, who censored all outgoing mail, certainly wouldn't pass that one. Of course, there were ways and means: one was to have two duplicate pages from two identical school atlases of your area of operations, in their case the Med – one for the folks at home and one for yourself – and then when you knew where you were bound you placed the letter over the map and pricked it with a pin on, say, Crete. After that all the old woman had to do was to put the letter on her own copy of the map, and hey presto, she knew all. Censoring officers didn't always spot pinpricks; but Pike was a petty officer with his rate to lose if they did, and anyway he didn't approve of such stratagems. 'Careless Talk Costs Lives' and 'Be Like Dad – Keep Mum'; that was what the posters said, and they were dead right.

At 2000 hours, with the day fading fast into night via the brief Mediterranean twilight period, the destroyer went to action stations, still maintaining her high speed. The engine sounds, the hum of the dynamos and the ventilators, the click-click of the gyro repeater on the compass platform and the ping of the Asdics as they kept up their relentless search for enemy submarines were the only sounds to break an intense and brooding silence. Overhead the stars began to show, hanging like millions of lanterns, so close overhead, it seemed, that a man could reach out and touch them. The whole sea was lit by them and from any enemy ship the destroyer must stand out clearly. The weather was being unkind: Sawbridge would have welcomed a blow from the Levant. The Med wasn't always like this, not even at this time of the year – far from it. But there was nothing he could do about it; and so far at any rate there didn't seem to be any other ships, their own or the Italians', moving in this sector. In the meantime the lookouts and all the bridge personnel were very much on the alert, while along the upper deck the guns' crews and the torpedomen stood by their weapons, ready for instant action.

Unknown to Sawbridge and his ship's company, events were moving towards a climax in the island of Crete. By the twenty-ninth of the previous month – April – something over fifty thousand troops had been evacuated from Greece to Crete, but soon after this control of the Aegean had passed to the Germans and Crete was very much under threat. It was impossible to re-equip the disarrayed British forces on the island; there was almost no air defence left, indeed no air presence that was of any account. The Mediterranean Fleet – since the Germans' supremacy in the air had made Suda Bay unusable – was forced to work from Alexandria, more than four hundred miles south. And on 20 May the main attack had come from the German land forces, airborne and immensely strong, against practically no opposition. As the twenty-second had dawned, Lord Louis Mountbatten's Fifth Destroyer Flotilla was not far off, while more destroyers were coming in from Alexandria and four cruisers with another three destroyers were patrolling off the north coast of the island, targets for vicious attack from the air. The cruisers *Gloucester* and *Fiji* came under very heavy attack in the Aegean and were sunk; previous to this, the cruiser *Naiad* had suffered severe bomb damage, the destroyer *Juno* had been sunk, and the Captain of HMS *Carlisle*, another cruiser, had been killed; while in the Kithera Channel, HMS *Warspite*, wearing the Force A Commander's flag, had been severely damaged in a bombing attack. Sawbridge was in fact steaming into an impossible position; and soon after midnight, as he came up towards the coast of Crete, he was able to pick up the sound of the never-ending aerial bombardment in the distance as the dive-bombers zoomed down on the defenceless troops in the north of the island. Although some thirty miles off the racket could be heard and the burning could be seen, the latter as a grotesque and devilish glow that lit the whole northern horizon when *Wharfedale*'s engines were stopped.

As Sawbridge remarked to Cameron, still awaiting his final orders, the south of the island appeared quiet.

'And thank God for it,' he said. 'Nervous, Sub?'

'Yes, sir.'

'I'm not surprised. It's always worse before it starts. If all goes well, we should make our contact soon.'

'How's it to be made, sir?'

'I don't know,' Sawbridge said. 'I wasn't entrusted with that knowledge! Actually, I don't believe the staff in Malta knew. I'm simply to be contacted, that's all, as I told the ship's company earlier.'

No more was said; they all waited, not knowing what they were waiting for. They waited for a whole nail-biting hour; and then, as Sawbridge paced the compass platform interminably, backwards and forwards, beneath the low-hanging stars, growing more and more impatient and anxious, a guarded voice from the starboard bridge lookout said: 'Something moving, sir, bearing green one-six-five ... distant about six cables, sir.'

Immediately Sawbridge swung his glasses on to the bearing and found his target: it looked like a small craft, possibly an inflatable dinghy, though he couldn't be certain. He swore beneath his breath; that dinghy could carry his contact, or it could carry an enemy with, for instance, limpet mines for fixing to his hull ... yet that would be unlikely, since the craft's occupants must know they would be seen. Limpet mines would be fixed by frogmen: he cursed himself for unhelpful thoughts. It had to be their contact.

It was.

Within the next thirty seconds a torch flashed briefly from the approaching craft; Sawbridge authorized no acknowledgement. He wouldn't take chances, preferred the occupant or occupants to make self-identification. As the craft came nearer he saw that it was indeed an inflatable dinghy, RAF pattern. In it were two men, ragged and dirty in the starlight, one of them carrying a large sack. Sawbridge leaned over the guardrail. 'Who are you?' he called down, his voice sounding unnatural and strained.

'Friends. You're expecting us, I think.' The voice was British, that of an officer unmistakably. 'My name's Gore-Lumley, Major, 3rd Hussars.'

'Right,' Sawbridge said, letting out a long breath of relief. 'Come aboard and for Christ's sake make it fast! Starboard side aft.' He turned, 'Number One, hands aft, pronto.'

Five minutes later the Hussar Major was on the compass platform with his sack-bearing companion, who turned out to be a Greek from the mainland, by name Orestis Kopoulos. He was bull-necked and barrel-chested, immensely tough and strong, with much hair covering a face like granite. Along with the sack he carried a sub-machine-gun, held across his body like a baby. He looked like a bandit and indeed, according to Gore-Lumley, was one.

'But a patriotic bugger,' the soldier said, grinning from a cork-blackened face. His clothing, which was highly unmilitary, was in tatters and he wore a bandage round his forehead. 'He detests all things German ... as a matter of fact he's a communist. Aren't you, Orestis, old chap?'

The bandit gave a big grin and said, 'Communist, yes.'

'But look here,' Sawbridge said, sounding puzzled, 'Russia's on the other side ... even if the signs are that she won't be for much longer. So how come a communist is assisting us, which I take it this man is?'

'He is,' Gore-Lumley answered. 'His Greek nationality comes before Russia, that's all. Greek first, communist second. As I said, he loathes Germans—'

'Nazis,' Kopoulos broke in, 'are swine.' He drew a hand across his throat, grinned again, and said, 'I kill them when I find them. Always.'

'That's the stuff,' Gore-Lumley said. 'Now, Captain. You'll want to know what your job is, I expect—'

'Right, I do. Fast, please, Major.'

'First a little of the background. You'll need that.' Gore-

36

Lumley rubbed at his eyes; he was obviously almost out on his feet, and was swaying as he spoke. 'So far most of the fighting's in the north, but it's due to move south – a number of our troops are moving down to Sphakia soon, I don't know quite when, ready to evacuate—'

'Has evacuation been ordered, Major?'

'No, not yet, but we all expect it. We just can't hold Crete, but the fact has yet to penetrate at home. Anyway, when the troops move down from Suda Bay, they're going to bring the bloody Hun with them, obviously. I repeat, I don't know when that'll happen but when it does, I've no doubt you'll be involved in the evacuation and you'll come under very intense attack—'

'In the meantime—'

'In the meantime there's this pick-up. I gather you don't know who it is?'

'No, I don't.'

Gore-Lumley grinned. 'It's a communist. A big one. Orestis Kopoulos' big white chief, actually. He's been given a guarantee of safety in return for services rendered. He wants to get back to Greece to carry on the fight there. I don't know if you'll be ordered to transport him, or whether he'll be transferred via Alexandria or Malta – that's largely up to you Naval johnnies, of course.' He added, 'There's a woman, too – his daughter. His name's Razakis, by the way, Stephanos Razakis, and he's something of a handful. Self-opinionated bastard, frankly – sorry, Orestis, but that's fact and you know it.'

Kopoulos grinned. 'I know it, yes.'

Sawbridge asked, 'Are you going to guide my party, Major?'

'I'm afraid not. I have to report elsewhere without delay – you won't be seeing me again. Orestis Kopoulos will guide your chaps, Captain. It's a longish trek ... and there's something else, I'm afraid.'

'Yes?'

Gore-Lumley said, 'Razakis – and this is why he wasn't able

37

to come with me – Razakis is being held by a platoon of Hun paratroops—'

Sawbridge caught the eye of his First Lieutenant and swore. 'I wasn't told this, Major!'

'No. Well, Razakis is a prisoner in his own stronghold, in a valley between the Idhi Oros and Levka Ori ranges. Your chaps'll have to fight through to him, then fight out again. They'll have to watch out for the Germans on the way – there's a force under a Colonel Heidrich in the south-west of the island – he's taken Cemetery Hill and Pink Hill already, and he's dug in south of the Canea-Maleme road. That's well west of Razakis, certainly, but you never know.'

'I'm going to need to land more men than I'd planned,' Sawbridge said. 'I've detailed twelve plus an officer, a PO and a leading-seaman—'

'Should be enough,' Gore-Lumley interrupted. 'I was going to recommend a small, fast, very uncluttered force, nothing that'll stand out.' Gore-Lumley paused, and twirled at his flamboyant moustache. 'We couldn't spare any troops and still can't. Every man's desperately needed to hold the coast till someone in Whitehall makes up his mind to evacuate. So I'm afraid it's all yours.'

4

MAJOR Gore-Lumley stressed that the landing-party must not look like the Royal Navy or any other disciplined fighting force but must be dressed in Cretan clothing to enable them to pass as indigenous banditry: hence the sack that had been brought aboard. In it would be found enough gear to give the necessary local colour, and it would help if faces were blackened like his own. This said, he re-embarked aboard his inflatable dinghy and vanished easterly across the water, heading obliquely for the shore. Orestis Kopoulos watched him until he was out of sight; the Greek was looking sombre. The two men seemed to be good friends. No time was lost in sorting out the dirty, smelly gear and in blackening faces, then the order was passed, quietly, from the compass platform: 'Away whaler!'

Cameron saw his men aboard quickly. As they slid down the falls he was thinking about his orders. According to Kopoulos, he faced something like a two-hour journey: four hours minimum before he could be back, and God knew how long it would take him to penetrate the German line, even though the enemy was present in no more than platoon strength according to Gore-Lumley. But dawn would be up within that four-hour minimum and Sawbridge had said that he could not risk his ship by being a sitting duck after dawn; this, Cameron fully understood. Sawbridge's intention was to take the destroyer to sea after the party had left and head south out of the area. He would come back in as soon as the light went again, but in addition would return during the day if the overall situation permitted. He would try to make it at noon; otherwise it would be 2000 hours. When Cameron made the shore on his return trip, he was to use the boat's Aldis to call the ship as soon as he had seen her – a portable, battery signalling lamp as provided for use in ships' boats was part of the landing-party's equipment. And the moment he made contact the whaler would go in to pick them all up....

Sawbridge leaned down as the whaler was reported ready to slip. 'Good luck, Sub. It's a tough assignment. Just do your best.'

'Yes, sir.' Cameron nodded to Petty Officer Pike and the order was given for the whaler to be slipped; down she went with a smack on to the still water. The bowman and stern-sheetsman bore off with boathooks and once the whaler, jammed to the gunwales with the men of the landing-party, was clear of the ship's side the crew pulled for the shore. They swept up to a shingle beach, already selected by reference to the chart and the Admiralty Sailing Directions for the area. There they lay off in a foot or so of water and Cameron ordered his party out. They waded ashore looking as brigand-ish as Kopoulos, and the whaler was despatched back to the destroyer.

It was a lonely, naked feeling.

Cameron didn't spend long dwelling on loneliness and the total cut-off from the comparative security of a warship. Time was valuable, and if he could make the earlier rendezvous, then so much the better. Every moment spent ashore would increase the danger. He spoke to Orestis Kopoulos. 'We're in your hands,' he said. 'That is, as regards the route.'

'Yes. And the rest, my British friend?'

Cameron met the Greek's eye squarely. 'For the rest, I'm in charge. If there's fighting, you must take your orders from me.'

Kopoulos laughed gently. 'I think I know more of fighting than you, my friend! I am a partisan, a guerrilla ... such

40

fighting is not the fighting of the British Navy with its big guns and its, what you call, bull, yes?'

'Yes,' Cameron answered, smiling but determined. 'All the same—'

'All the same – yes. I understand.' Kopoulos reached out a hand, and Cameron took it. The Greek gripped him like a vice. He went on, 'You give the orders, my friend, I give the advice. Only a fool would refuse that. I do not think you look like a fool.'

'Thanks,' Cameron said, grinning. 'That seems a pretty good arrangement to me.'

'Then it is agreed.' Kopoulos looked up the shore, silvery beneath the moon and stars, those splendid but unfriendly lanterns that shone on massive rock behind the beach. Gesturing the seamen to follow, he moved away from the water, taking long, loping strides. Cameron moved up to walk alongside him. Petty Officer Pike fell in behind, while Leading-Seaman Wellington brought up the rear behind the junior ratings, two of whom were carrying the box of grenades. Once clear of the beach they began climbing. It was a tough climb; but the Greek seemed to know every inch of the way, every jut of the rock, every crevice. They moved in silence apart from occasional brief directions from Kopoulos. Cameron wondered if he had been too officious, too pompous perhaps, in his insistence on command; Kopoulos, that man of obvious experience, was a good deal older than himself and knew his own country. Cameron had no doubt sounded brash; on the other hand, the responsibility was his, and Pike and the seamen would expect their own officer to be in charge: already Cameron had heard mutterings from some of the hands, men who didn't go much on being entrusted to the care of a Greek communist who could for all they knew be in the pay of Russia, Adolf Hitler's curious bedfellow. Russia was the enemy, and communists couldn't be trusted. That, Cameron believed, was the feeling as the climb finished on more level ground. After a while Kopoulos became more talkative and asked about the progress of the war at sea. Cameron was

non-committal, not knowing how far he should go in impart-
ing such information as he possessed, which in fact was
little enough. Neither the Admiralty nor the various
Commanders-in-Chief were accustomed to confide in sub-
lieutenants ... Countering the questions, he asked Kopoulos
if he knew the originator of the guarantee apparently given to
Stephanos Razakis.

'Yes,' Kopoulos said. 'Yes, I know this.'

'Can you tell me who?'

'Yes,' Kopoulos said again. 'Churchill.'

The journey was made without any interference along the
way. They were now in well wooded country. No Germans
appeared to be in the vicinity, and they didn't meet any
Cretans either; no doubt they were all lying low while the war
swept over their island – all except the partisans from Greece,
anyway. Cameron pondered on Churchill's involvement;
Churchill's motto should have been, like the Royal Artillery,
ubique. Not that he was here in person, of course, but his great
looming personality seemed to have arrived for the succour of
a partisan of importance; and now the very name of Winston
Churchill had the effect of making this whole mission into one
of much greater significance. Success had more than ever to
be achieved; but Cameron was under no illusions as to the
odds against him. Not only had he to penetrate the German
line twice, but he had to get Razakis to the coast and then hide
him away until Sawbridge brought the destroyer back in. That
would be difficult once the escape was known. And the fact
that Sawbridge had been doubtful about the noon rendezvous
could point to at least a couple of imponderables weighing on
his mind: the whole south coast might be aflame by then as the
British, Australian and New Zealand Armies moved south for
Sphakia; or Sawbridge might have received new orders.
Wharfedale's next duty was to reinforce Lord Louis Mountbatten's flotilla off Canea in the Aegean and then, according
to Gore-Lumley, probably to assist in the massive evacuation
operation. If events should suddenly start to move faster,

even Winston Churchill's wishes might be considered expendable; sub-lieutenants and landing-parties certainly were.

It was some ten minutes short of the estimated two hours since leaving the beach behind them that Orestis Kopoulos laid a hand on Cameron's arm and said, 'Now we take special care.'

'We're there?'

'Almost, yes.'

Cameron looked at the luminous dial of his wrist-watch. 'We've made good time.'

'Yes ... H. Samuel time!'

'What?'

Kopoulos grinned. 'A joke. The commercials broadcast by Radio Normandy in the days of the peace, you remember?'

'I remember.' The sudden remembrance brought back scenes of home, of Aberdeen before he had joined up. It brought back that Sunday morning, so long ago it seemed now, when at 1100 hours the voice of Neville Chamberlain had announced, almost with tears in it, that this country was now at war with Germany ... Cameron jerked himself back to the present. 'How far to go now, Kopoulos?'

'Half a mile, perhaps a little less. The night is very still. Listen and you will hear something.'

They all kept very silent. At first Cameron could hear nothing beyond his own breathing, the thump of his own heart. Then he began to pick up sounds: distant, but distinct in the still air of the night. Footsteps, measured ones, steel-shod heels banging into hard ground.

'You hear, my friend?'

Cameron nodded. 'Yes. German sentries?'

'Yes. The perimeter ... listen more.'

Cameron did so, with Petty Officer Pike beside him now, fingering his revolver. New sounds came, metallic sounds, sounds like the snick of rifle bolts and the small noises from the equipment of men on the move. Pike said in a hoarse whisper, 'The bastards are closing in on us, sir.'

Kopoulos caught the remark. He said, 'Yes, that is right. But we are in good cover, so—'

'They must have heard us,' Cameron interrupted.

'Not so. It is a routine patrol, a probe to satisfy the German Commander, that is all. I say again, we are in good cover, my friend. It is my advice that we remain in it, very still, very quiet, down on our stomachs beneath the brushwood until we see what is happening. You will give the order, please?'

'Good advice,' Cameron said. He passed the word back to all hands to get down flat, conceal themselves, and make no sound or movement. They waited; the sounds came closer to the hidden men, apparently coming towards them from their right. Cameron's own breathing was like a dead give-away in his ears, something that surely cried out to be heard. The minutes ticked past; crunching footsteps came closer and voices could soon be heard plainly, and some laughter. Cameron almost jumped a mile when once again Kopoulos laid a hand on his arm. The Greek spoke with his mouth hard up against Cameron's ear. 'They will pass across our front, I think. And I think we must attack.'

'Why? Why show ourselves, Kopoulos?'

'Because to kill them reduces their strength, for one thing. For another, their uniforms and weapons may be helpful to us, my friend.'

'But they'll give the alarm!'

'No. Not if we are very quick. And we outnumber them, I believe. To me, the sounds speak of four men only.' Kopoulos gave a low laugh. 'My ears are well-trained in such matters, and I do not doubt them.'

'Yes, but—'

'I think we should attack. That is my advice. You will give the order, please?' The voice had hardened now and meant to have its way. 'As they pass before us, while their backs are turned, I shall kill the NCO in charge. Immediately, your men will attack the other three, and silence them. You understand?'

Cameron said, 'Seaman are not commandos, Kopoulos.

44

They don't know the drill. It won't be their fault, but they'll bungle it.' He paused. 'I'm sorry, Kopoulos. There won't be any attack.'

'Then you are a fool.'

'So I'm a fool, Kopoulos,' Cameron said.

'And a coward.'

Cameron held on to his temper; cowardice didn't come into it. What he had said had been nothing but the truth. Ratings in destroyers had never been trained in any kind of hand-to-hand combat, let alone in the technique of attack that had to be so sudden and unannounced that the target didn't get a chance even to shout a warning. If they went into that sort of attack now, the game would be up and Stephanos Razakis would remain right where he was. Steadily Cameron said, 'There will be no attack, Kopoulos. We keep hidden.'

There was a hiss of fury from the Greek, but no more argument. The Germans were too close by this time; and half a minute later they were in full view as they pushed through trees and undergrowth little more than inches from where the British party lay concealed. The moonlight fell upon their uniforms, glinted off the metal of their weapons. Kopoulos had been dead right: there were four men, one of them an NCO. Sudden blinding pain came to Cameron as a hard and heavy heel crunched down on his outstretched, brushwood-covered hand, biting into its back. He made no sound; the effort not to cry out was considerable. As the German patrol moved away, still talking and laughing, he found sweat pouring from him in streams.

Off the south coast, the destroyer waited for the dawn; Sawbridge had remained on the compass platform throughout, sometimes pacing, sometimes hunched in a corner. He had brooded on whether or not he should take his command to sea, to get as much distance between the ship and any German air attack as possible, before the dawn showed in the eastern sky. Cameron couldn't possibly be back before that dawn in the normal run of events, so much was certain. But something

45

might go wrong and the landing-party might need to beat a retreat back to the ship. If that happened, then they must find the destroyer waiting as they expected. That much risk had to be accepted. Sawbridge turned as he heard a step on the ladder, and saw his First Lieutenant.

He said, 'Hullo there, Number One.'

'Let me take over, sir. Just till dawn.'

Suddenly, Sawbridge gave a yawn, a big one. He smiled and said, 'It's not a bad idea at that. I'll need to be bright and fresh when we move out ... bright-eyed and bushy-tailed as the Yanks say, I believe.'

Drummond said sourly, 'It's a pity they aren't saying it here, sir.'

'Oh, they'll come in one day, Number One,' Sawbridge said. 'When they're good and ready, they'll come in. I don't blame them for putting off the day – it was never their war in the first place.' He read the disagreement in his First Lieutenant's face, but one had to be fair. He left the compass platform to snatch an hour or two of sleep. He didn't get it; the Germans saw to that. The moment Sawbridge's head touched the pillow the alarm rattlers sounded and he went back, at the double, to the compass platform. As he went, he heard the screaming crescendo of the dive-bombers, who seemed to be concentrating their attack on the harbour installations, primitive as they were, of Sphakia. Fires lit the sky, and chunks of masonry could be seen spinning up into the air as the bombs fell.

'They must have got Gore-Lumley's buzz,' Sawbridge said, 'about the troops moving to the south. This is the reception committee. I'll take her out, Number One, and get her zig-zagging.' He turned to the Officer of the Watch. 'Engines to full ahead, wheel amidships. Course, one-eight-oh degrees.' He stared out over the land, at the ferocious scene as the Stukas struck again and again.

Wharfedale went to sea, with all despatch. As she went the dive-bombers came in, two of them at first, screaming down from the night sky on either beam. Sawbridge ordered the helm hard over to starboard, then hard a-port; the destroyer weaved desperately between the falling bombs, her three-inch anti-aircraft gun and close range weapons putting up a murderous barrage as she went. One of the dive-bombers came right smack into the fire from the port pom-pom: the aircraft's windscreen fragmented and the pilot spurted blood. The destroyer raced away under full power of her shafts as the German hit the sea and exploded her bomb-load on impact; another came in to take her place. As the destroyer's decks all but vanished under the flung spray of the near misses, the RNVR midshipman came from the W/T office to the compass platform with a cyphered message already broken down into plain language. It was prefaced 'Most Urgent' and was brief.

'Read it to me, snotty,' Sawbridge said.

'Aye, aye, sir. From Commander-in-Chief, sir ... previous orders in abeyance. You are to proceed with the utmost despatch to rendezvous with main Fleet units off southern-most point of Scarpanto.'

'That's all?'

'Yes, sir.'

Sawbridge blew out a long breath. 'Course, oh-nine-oh,' he said to the Officer of the Watch. Then he added more or less to himself, 'And God help Cameron's party.'

Expendability was in the air now.

5

ORESTIS KOPOULOS was indulging himself in a fit of the sulks; he was averse to having his advice disregarded. The Germans had gone now; Cameron tried to make his peace with the Greek.

'I'm sorry,' he said. 'I don't mean to sound ungrateful, Kopoulos. But what you suggested just wasn't on.'

'Tell that to Churchill,' the Greek said, 'when you report to him that you have lost Stephanos Razakis.' He thumped himself on his chest, which was a massive one. 'I, Orestis Kopoulos, accept no blame. I wash my hands. You understand, Englishman?'

Cameron said patiently, 'No one's blaming you. And we're going to get Razakis out. To do it, I still need your help.'

'Yes.'

'You'll give it, then?'

The Greek made no immediate answer. A black scowl was visible in the moonlight filtering through the trees; he moved away by himself, with an arrogant swing of his shoulders. Petty Officer Pike said, 'Now you've gone and done it, sir!'

'D'you think I was wrong?' Cameron asked.

'No, sir, that I don't. But God knows what the next step is, if Kopoulos doesn't co-operate.'

'He will,' Cameron said. 'He won't let Razakis down.'

Pike made a sound of assent. 'I expect you're right, sir.'

Cameron was; Kopoulos came back through the trees and though still appearing angry said, 'You will have my help, of course. I have my loyalties.'

'Thank you, Kopoulos,' Cameron said.

'What,' the Greek asked, 'do you propose to do?'

'Close the German perimeter. You agree?'

Kopoulos gave a sardonic laugh. 'If we do not do that,' he said, 'we shall come no closer to Razakis! Yes – I agree. And when we get within sight of the perimeter, we shall remain in cover until I have watched and seen and made an assessment. Do you agree to that?'

Cameron grinned. 'Come off it, Kopoulos! We'll get nowhere if we each try to score off the other. Let's forget it, shall we?'

He reached out a hand; after some hesitation Kopoulos took it and gave it a hard grip. 'Yes, we shall forget. You have much to learn, my friend, but you stand by what you believe to be right. That is good, I think – at least, sometimes. Now we are good allies again. Let us move on.'

They did so, with extreme caution, going dead slow so as to minimize any sound that might reach the German perimeter. It was an eerie, scaring advance through the night. The sound of the patrolling sentries' footsteps came louder as they approached, and other sounds came from near at hand – the dry scurryings of small disturbed animals, the cries of birds. Cameron, worried by the bird sounds, asked Kopoulos in a whisper if this would be likely to alert the Germans.

'I believe not,' Kopoulos answered. 'The Nazis are too stupid, too cocksure as well. They believe Crete is already theirs in any case and that no one would be so foolish as to creep, like us, into the interior, far from the sea.'

'What makes you think that?'

'My heart,' Kopoulos said briefly. 'And because I know the Nazis. Once, I was in their hands, but escaped.' He said no more; they moved on. After some more progress Kopoulos advised that they should advance on their stomachs; Cameron passed the order back via Petty Officer Pike. Another hundred yards or so and they had the German position in view. Already Kopoulos had described it: it was a natural fortification beyond the tree-line, until now the home and operational base of the partisan leader and thus well-known to Kopoulos. In fact it consisted of little more than a pattern of great rocks clustered on rising ground, a perfect defensive position that had succumbed only to the German artillery. The damage caused by the heavy guns could be seen clearly in the moonlight; according to Kopoulos, Razakis and his daughter had remained safe in their personal strongpoint below ground, protected by the great rock formation itself, but had been captured when the German soldiers had stormed in behind the rifles and bayonets after the gunfire had softened up the position. Sadly, a large number of the partisans, fine fighters all, had been slaughtered in the bombardment. All this had been only a matter of days ago; Cameron could almost imagine he smelled the gunsmoke and the spilled blood.

Kopoulos had also said that he knew a secret way into the stronghold, but that by this time the Germans would almost without a doubt have discovered it for themselves.

'Nevertheless,' he said now, 'it may still be the best place to use. Perhaps the only one. You can see for yourself the great difficulty of frontal attack.'

Cameron could: under that high, bright moon, and the stars that still shone down, no one could hope to climb up to the rocks without being spotted. As they watched, the German sentries could be seen marching their posts – two men with kneeboots and steel helmets, carrying 7.9-mm KAR-98K infantry rifles, one patrolling the perimeter to the east, the other to the west, and meeting at a central point opposite the hidden British seamen. Behind, between the rocks, other men could be seen standing-to with the moonlight glinting from their weapons.

On the face of it, it looked hopeless.

Cameron glanced at Petty Officer Pike, who was lying full stretch beside him. 'What d'you think?' he asked.

'Bloody suicide, sir, that's what I think. We'd never reach half-way ... not alive we wouldn't.'

Cameron nodded. 'You've probably never said a truer

word!' He turned to Orestis Kopoulos. 'Where's this secret entry of yours?'

Kopoulos lifted a hand cautiously and pointed. 'Over there, my friend, to the right. A tunnel. The entry is in the trees. The tunnel emerges in the centre of the rocks.'

'Man-made?'

Kopoulos shook his head. 'No. It is a natural passage, formed by the natural disturbances of the earth millions of years ago, when the rocks themselves were cast up where now they stand. It is of immense strength, so—'

'So it won't have been damaged by the artillery bombardment?'

'Damage is unlikely, I think. But as I have said, the Nazis will have found it, and—'

'But as you also said, Kopoulos, it could be the only way in. And there's another point, isn't there?'

'What point, my friend?' Kopoulos's questioning eyes seemed liquid black in the moonlight.

'This: the German guns caused other damage ... the tunnel's exit could have been covered by the broken rock, couldn't it? In which case, the Germans may never have found it.'

Kopoulos grinned. 'This is possible. But if it has happened, then the exit is no more. It will be totally blocked by the rock fall!'

'I suppose so.' Cameron felt his face flushing: there had been patient scorn in the Greek's voice. The Englishman's mental processes, the tone had said, were far from fast or bright. Difficulties, however, existed only to be overcome: Cameron had had that point made to him in the *King Alfred*. It was an officer's responsibility to find a way and to overcome all obstacles. Another piece of good advice from the past came to mind: don't cross bridges till you come to them. He said crisply, 'That needn't necessarily be the case, though. That is, we can at least have a go at entering. If we're blocked off, then we'll have to retreat and think again. Right, Kopoulos?'

'Perhaps, yes. But we do not rush, like bulls at gates as you would say.'

'Then—'

'We use our heads. We fool the Nazis. It is easily done, my English friend!'

'How?'

'We make a feint. A diversion of their attention. It has been done before.'

Cameron said cynically, 'Too bloody many times! It's old hat, Kopoulos. We won't fool them that way.'

'Not so. Always the Nazis are fooled by the same things. It is in their stupid nature. They act like automatons, without thought, producing the same reactions time after time. You will see.'

Cameron said, 'Well, the sooner the better, Kopoulos. We've around two hours now to dawn. And I still want to make that noon rendezvous off Sphakia,' he added. True, that was as yet ten hours ahead; but it didn't seem as though the German-held strongpoint was going to be penetrated quickly, and if they were successful in extracting Razakis and the girl, they might well have to fight a rearguard action all the way back to the coast, and at best that was going to slow them up. Kopoulos expounded his plan: it was simple enough; too simple in Cameron's view. Four of the seamen were to be ordered to crawl round to the western side of the rocks while Kopoulos, with Cameron and the remainder of the party, moved eastwards towards the tunnel entry. The western party was to allow ten minutes for Kopoulos to get into position, and then one of the men was to show himself briefly. Once the German garrison had reacted, all four were to open as rapid a fire as possible from the cover of the trees. When the first shots were heard from the phoney western attack, Kopoulos would start to penetrate the tunnel.

Cameron said, 'In the absence of anything better, we'll give it a try.'

'Do not disparage, my friend! I tell you, the Nazis will do just as I expect them to do.' Kopoulos sounded fully confident, and was smiling happily as action approached; basically, he was a fighter, at his best, Cameron fancied, when the bullets began to fly towards his hated Nazis. Cameron made his dispositions quickly: Leading-Seaman Wellington was detailed to take three men and the box of grenades round to the west, with orders to pick off as many Germans as he could during the feint and make the thing to that extent real and useful. Petty Officer Pike would go with the main attack. The orders passed, no time was lost in moving out. Orestis Kopoulos slithered along fast with his sub-machine-gun, followed by Cameron and the others, while Leading-Seaman Wellington crawled out to the west after watches had been synchronized. Cameron and his seamen were forced to move fast, dangerously so Cameron thought, in order to keep Kopoulos within sight; but their movement didn't appear to have been seen by the troops in the strongpoint.

It was seen by someone outside, however.

As Cameron closed towards the tunnel entry behind Orestis Kopoulos, he saw a grotesque sight: in the moonlight a fat, bespectacled German soldier stood, wrapped in a greatcoat draped with belts and pouches, his mouth open in sudden terror, a half-eaten sausage still in his right hand. The mouth was obviously about to utter a shout of warning, or more likely a scream, when Kopoulos went into fast action. Dropping the sub-machine-gun, he flung himself on the German sentry and got steely fingers around the throat. Then, holding the man's mouth tightly against his chest, Kopoulos reached behind his body and brought a short knife from his waistband. Quick as lightning his hand moved to the German's back, and the knife plunged in. It must have been razor-sharp: the movement had looked easy, like a knife going into butter, and the German made no sound at all as he died.

Kopoulos got to his feet, stared down at the body and gave it a kick. 'A good Nazi,' he said. 'A dead one!'

'And it means they've found the tunnel, Kopoulos.'

'Yes,' the Greek agreed, 'and it means also that it is unblocked, I think. Luck is with us, my friend!' He looked at his wrist-watch. 'Two minutes, then if all goes well we enter.'

The seconds ticked away; Cameron's attention now was on the hands of his watch. He felt a curious sensation in his guts: the entry was going to be a bloody business, there could be no doubt about that at all. They wouldn't all get away with it. The two minutes passed ... now, Leading-Seaman Wellington would be showing himself, briefly. More seconds went by; half a minute passed. Both Cameron and Kopoulos were on edge now; Cameron felt sweat run down his face. Had something gone wrong, or were the Germans simply not as alert as they should be?

Then it came.

At first there was just a single shot. After that, the strongpoint came alive. There were shouted orders, cries of alarm, a small searchlight flashed on, its finger weaving out over the trees beyond. Then came the firing: a number of rifles crashed out from the strongpoint and were answered from the trees. After this, the explosions of four or five grenades were heard. Cameron snapped, 'Right, in we go!'

Already Kopoulos was moving for the tunnel entrance, just behind the dead body of the fat German, its spectacles still upon the nose but now broken and pathetic-looking ... that body had been someone's son, possibly someone's husband, someone's father. But there was no time for such thoughts now. Behind Kopoulos, with the nine seamen moving in ahead of Petty Officer Pike, Cameron plunged blind into the tunnel, feeling for his footholds and keeping his arms in front of his face as protection against whatever he might bump into. There could be danger in using a torch, or the boat's Aldis being borne along by the signalman, if any light was seen from the other end; they just had to hope and pray and trust in Orestis Kopoulos. At first the tunnel floor sloped steeply and the advance became a tumbling, headlong rush in which men cursed viciously as they hit against roof and sides and were lashed at by unnamed things growing or hanging or protruding from the sides. The rush eased as the floor levelled out.

Then, after running level for some way, the upward climb began and the advance was slowed even more.

Soon, some sort of light was seen ahead. That light came and went, flickering and fading, and distantly the sound of the rifles was heard again. The light was probably the rifle flashes, overlaid by the weaving of the searchlight. In any case, it meant they had the end of the tunnel in their sights now. Cameron cannoned into Kopoulos, who had stopped.

'For God's sake!' Cameron snapped, his nerves playing him up badly.

'We are nearly there,' Kopoulos said unnecessarily. 'I shall go first. My gun is the best we have between us, and will cause the most alarm and surprise.' Cameron didn't argue the point; the Greek was undoubtedly right. Kopoulos got on the move again and within another half-minute crammed on speed and came out from the exit, right into the heart of the strongpoint, with his sub-machine-gun blazing from a crouching position just clear enough of the exit to allow the rest of the party to emerge and join in with their rifles.

The Germans, as Kopoulos had predicted, had been caught right on the hop, taken utterly by surprise, wonderfully fooled by sheer, old-hat simplicity. The first gunfire went slap into their backs as they crowded a makeshift firing-step by the summit of the westward-facing rocks. A number of dead men hurtled down, colandered by the Greek's sub-machine-gun fire, to fetch up bloodily on the rock floor. As other men ran in from left and right, the Greek swung his gun in a murderous arc of fire, his eyes narrowed and glinting, and Cameron and the naval ratings pumped bullets into any German that came into their range, firing virtually point-blank into the field-grey uniforms. Cameron felt a slight burning sensation in the flesh of his left upper arm, just below the shoulder, and thought little of it, quite unconscious of the pouring blood. From the corner of his eye he saw two of his seamen fall; then, as the fighting continued all around him, four figures swept over the summit from the west: Leading-Seaman Wellington and his hands, firing down into the centre, picking off the remaining Germans one by one. A chance shot going upwards from the defenders took one of the naval party, and the body fell, streaming blood from the throat, to end as the Germans had ended, on the rock.

Cameron dashed sweat from his eyes and looked around as the firing faltered and fell away. Kopoulos was now laying about himself with his knife, driving it into chests and backs, slitting the throats of cowed men. As he was thus occupied, Cameron saw a German officer, a *hauptmann* he believed, coming towards him with a white handkerchief held above his head and the other arm hanging limp at his side. Cameron called out to Kopoulos.

'They're surrendering, Kopoulos. Leave them.'

A Greek word came back at him, obviously a four-letter one. Kopoulos carried on with his bloody work. Cameron shouted, 'Put down that knife, Kopoulos! We don't fight on after a surrender. Drop it or I'll have you disarmed.' He caught the eye of Petty Officer Pike, and nodded. Pike took his meaning, moved for Kopoulos and, with surprisingly wiry strength, pinioned his arms. Kopoulos raved for a while, but then slackened and dropped the bloodied knife.

He said, 'Yes, you are right and I am sorry. You English have your ways ... and your orders. Me, I have suffered torture from the Nazis – but yes, you are right. I stop now.'

Cameron blew out his breath in relief. 'We'd better find Razakis pronto,' he said. 'There could be other Germans in the vicinity. I'd rather not hang around.' He turned to the German officer, who had halted a few paces away and stood with a British rifle nudging his backbone. He asked, 'Do you speak English?'

'A little,' the German answered.

'Where is Razakis, and his daughter?'

The German hesitated. Cameron said, 'I've not much time. If necessary, I'll get Kopoulos to make you answer. I dare say you can guess what that will mean.'

The threat alone did the trick; the German officer shrugged

and capitulated, looking nervously towards the Greek. Kopoulos seemed to be known to him, if only, perhaps, by reputation. The *hauptmann* swallowed, muttered something in German, then told Cameron to follow him. Cameron did so, gesturing the rating with the rifle to continue covering his prisoner. Kopoulos joined them as they followed the German. He asked in a rough voice, 'Where are you leading the Englishman, Nazi swine?'

'To Razakis ...'

'Yes? Is he not in his cave below?'

'No, he is not there—'

'Yet that would be the most secure place to hold him, I think! Do not forget that I know this place well, Nazi. Do you take me for a fool?' The Greek's voice rose in anger. 'Where is Razakis? Is he dead? Or do you intend to lead me and my English friends into an ambush? Is that it?'

'I am sorry.' The German spoke stiffly, his face wearing a wooden look now. 'I do not know what you mean. There is no ambush, and Razakis lives. The daughter also.'

'Then before you lead the way anywhere, Nazi, tell me where Razakis is.'

The officer said, 'He is outside the strongpoint. The strong-point was at risk—'

'Because this was where we would expect to find Razakis – yes! So you moved him.' Kopoulos once again brought out his knife and laid the point against the German's throat. 'Have a care that you do not lead us astray, Nazi. Now move.'

The German moved; Kopoulos, shouldering the naval rating out of the way, moved behind him, drawing his knife round the neck until the point was just below the hair-line at the back. Keeping close, he and Cameron followed, making through the close-set rocks towards a track that ran down in a northerly direction, heading away into mountainous country, excellent terrain in which to hide a wanted man, real bandit country by the look of it, stark and empty beneath the all-seeing moon.

They didn't reach the track.

They had gone only some half-dozen paces when a high scream came, as though from under their feet, from the very bowels of the earth, a scream of purest pain, shrill – a woman's scream torn from the throat as though by physical torture beyond all endurance.

6

EVERYTHING seemed to be in a state of flux: the Fleet and the land forces had been badly caught out by the sheer size and ferocity of the German onslaught on Crete; and the RAF seemed to have gone out of existence, to the disgust of the men on land and water. As *Wharfedale* headed on her easterly course to rendezvous off the island of Scarpanto with the heavy Mediterranean Fleet units – for what possible purpose, Sawbridge and his officers had no idea whatsoever – a cancellation of those orders came via the W/T office in another signal in naval cypher: *Wharfedale* was to reverse her course and was now to rendezvous with the Fifth Destroyer Flotilla, currently withdrawing at speed from the Aegean towards Alexandria.

'Back to first base,' Sawbridge said. 'That was what we came for in the first place!' He joined the navigating officer at the chart table and tried to work out a time and place for the rendezvous: there was in fact precious little information to go on, and Sawbridge could only anticipate that the rendezvous position would be anywhere he cared to guess between his present position and the south-western tip of Crete beyond Sphakia. As he said to Bradley, it all depended on the speed of the Fifth Flotilla and he could only make the assumption that they would be proceeding at their maximum. On the other hand, it was unlikely they would have left the Aegean without coming under attack and all or any of the destroyers could well have sustained damage that would cut their speed.

Sawbridge said edgily, 'Damn signal could have been a shade more precise ... having been made at all, I doubt if any security would have been shattered by adding a little more gen.' He scanned the chart again, then sighed and said, 'All right, Pilot, bring her round on the reciprocal.'

'Aye, aye, sir.'

The orders were given and *Wharfedale* came round hard to port, her rails going under on the turn. Sawbridge paced the compass platform moodily. Command was fine, but could be a two-edged sword. Unless orders were precise, you were left to assess, which largely meant guess, for yourself – like now. You stood a fifty-fifty chance of being wrong every time, and then the Admiralty dropped on you like a ton of bricks. Nevertheless, there were bright spots: Sawbridge, and for that matter all his ship's company, would be glad enough to join up with Captain (D)5 as Lord Louis Mountbatten's appointment was known officially. The Fifth Flotilla was something of a crack formation, welded into a fine fighting team by their Captain (D); it would be an honour to be part of it, even if the constantly changing orders should leave them there only for a short time.

Sawbridge stopped his restless pacing and stared around the horizons through his binoculars. No enemy in sight, on the sea or in the air. So far, so good. The dawn was not so far off now; Cameron was much on Sawbridge's mind and he aired his thoughts to his First Lieutenant.

'0400,' he said as the watch changed. 'Cameron's party should be on their way back, I should think.'

'If they haven't been cut up, sir.'

'Oh, don't be a bloody defeatist, Number One! We have to assume they'll make the rendezvous.'

'The new orders could help in the pick-up,' Drummond said. 'Purely fortuitous ... but we'll be rather nearer Sphakia at noon than we would have been if we'd continued to Scarpanto.'

Sawbridge nodded. 'A similar thought did cross my mind too. But it'll depend on Lord Louis – and *his* orders.'

Drummond agreed, but added, 'Lord Louis always gives a chap a sporting chance, sir. And he's human.'

'Maybe, but war's war after all. Anyway, I'll ask permission to detach. Lord Louis may have some knowledge of this man Razakis, who's said to be so ruddy important!'

Wharfedale rushed on, still under full power and flinging back an immense bow-wave as the dawn stole up from the east behind them, from way beyond Scarpanto and the German air bases at the island's southern tip. Probably, Sawbridge thought, those air bases had had something to do with the movement of the heavy ships with which he had been ordered previously to rendezvous; the force may well have included Cunningham's aircraft-carriers, while the main armament of the battleships could deliver some devastating broadsides on to those airfields ...

At a little before 0700 hours the masthead lookout reported ships ahead, hull down on the horizon as yet and unidentifiable. Sawbridge immediately pressed the alarm rattlers, bringing up the watch below to join the watch on deck at full action stations. By now their position on the chart was almost due south of Cape Krio at Crete's south-western tip – west now of Sphakia. They hadn't any land in sight and if the ships were Lord Louis's, then he too was keeping well clear of the island and no blame to him for that. On the iron-deck, Mr Vibart stood by his torpedo-tubes and shaded his eyes ahead and to port towards the approaching ships. Soon, as they came fast towards the *Wharfedale*, he was able to make an identification. 'Destroyers, Charlie,' he said to his Torpedo-Gunner's Mate.

'Lord Louis, sir?'

'Right,' Vibart said. '*Kelly, Kipling* and *Kashmir* ... I'd know 'em anywhere.' A moment later the compass platform confirmed the identification over the tannoy, and action stations were fallen out, back to second degree of readiness. Vibart, feeling conversational, said, 'Lord Louis ... I served under him once, or did I tell you before now?'

'Yes,' the TGM answered, grinning. 'You did an' all!'

'Back in 1934,' Mr Vibart went on with a touch of wistfulness, not to be silenced in the retelling for the umpteenth time. 'In the old *Daring*. Good days, they were. Lord Louis, he was a lad all right! I was an LTO then ... but the skipper talked to me like I was an officer. Knew all the lads' names, where they come from, whether they was married or not.' He fell silent, pondering on past peacetime glories before the Navy had become ninety per cent reserves and hostilities-only ratings, some of whom were wet as scrubbers and didn't even know how to tie a cap ribbon with a decent bow, or how to wear their black silks, a proper shower .. by now *Wharfedale* was manoeuvring to join the flotilla and come up in rear of the column. Mr Vibart watched as the ship swept up on the port bow of the leader, HMS *Kelly*, passing close now. He stared across the water towards the leader's compass platform: Lord Louis was there all right, you could always tell him, like the late Admiral Beatty, by the set of his cap, which was itself of a slightly different pattern from those of ordinary officers, hard to place the difference but it was there all right, kind of individualistic. The Captain (D) was in the fore part of the compass platform, smiling and talking and watching the *Wharfedale*, as she swept past with her bosun's calls piping in salute to the Senior Officer. Lord Louis returned the hand salute of *Wharfedale*'s captain and almost involuntarily Mr Vibart's right hand also went to the brim of his cap in personal tribute to his old skipper, who really didn't look all that much older. Lord Louis, Captain RN now and cousin of the King, or something like that anyway, and he could talk to any rating, man to man and no bull. Pity the whole Navy wasn't like that; Mr Vibart shook his head sadly as his hand came down from the salute, and he busied himself by a little hazing of his torpedomen, who were sometimes a bloody lazy bunch ...

On the bridge, the signal lamps were busy. A welcome was being sent across from Captain (D) before *Wharfedale* had put her helm over to take station in line ahead: I DID NOT REALLY NEED YOU BUT AM DELIGHTED TO HAVE YOU. AM PROCEED-

Drummond was grinning as the Yeoman of Signals read off
the message from his pad. 'Didn't really want us . . . it smacks
of a cock-up somewhere!'

Sawbridge nodded. 'It wouldn't be the first time, Number
One. Fleet Signal Office at Alex . . . however, there's a bright
spot – if Lord Louis does get orders for Sphakia, we'll be back
where Cameron needs us, and with luck we'll even make the
noon rendezvous.' He sounded greatly relieved.

Drummond asked, 'Are you going to put it to Captain (D),
sir?'

'Yes. I'll summarize my orders.' Sawbridge turned to the
Yeoman and dictated an informative signal, asking permission to keep to his rendezvous with the landing-party. Soon a
reply came back: permission was granted if circumstances
permitted nearer noon. There was a good deal of background
information as well; Lord Louis was a believer in keeping his
ships' companies in the picture. The situation in the north of
Crete had become hopeless, with the troops in Suda Bay
virtually out of vital supplies that it was not possible to replen-
ish; the continual bombing had put the port out of the reckoning as a supply base although the cruiser-minelayer *Abdiel*
and a handful of destroyers had performed miracles. Things
were not going too well.

And, in the immediate and local sense at any rate, matters
were to get sadly worse. At a little before 0800 hours, with the
Fifth Flotilla some forty miles off Crete, the German dive-
bombers were seen roaring in from the north-east. As they
approached, the anti-aircraft umbrella went up, the tremendous din of it threatening to split ear-drums. The whole sky
was peppered with bursting shrapnel; the pom-poms kept up
a continuous barrage and as the Stukas roared down at their
immense speeds the Oerlikons blasted away at them, the men
in the straps almost turning somersaults as they strove to
elevate enough to hit the screaming dive-bombers and their
iron-faced, goggled pilots. But nothing could keep those

bombers at bay: almost as soon as the attack had come in, *Kashmir* had been hit and sunk, going down almost immediately the bombs blasted her; then *Kelly* was hit with her helm hard-a-starboard and, moving through the death-filled water at thirty knots, turned over to float for a while upside down until she sank to the bottom.

At once, *Kipling* was seen to be going in to pick up survivors. Sawbridge passed the orders to take *Wharfedale* in to her assistance. *Kipling* was moving in a hail of bombs from the Stukas, moving bravely and steadily in towards the swimming groups of men; soon *Wharfedale* also was under ferocious and sustained attack, with great gouts of water from near misses drenching her decks. The officers and men on her compass platform stared in horror as they saw a change in the tactics of some of the Stukas: the German pilots were swooping in now to machine-gun the survivors in the water. There were cries of fury and frustration from *Wharfedale*'s decks as the men, hit by the streaking bullets, threw up their arms and vanished beneath the water. A moment later, *Wharfedale* was hit aft.

A count was made of casualties: fifteen men at the after guns, on the searchlight platform and at the torpedo-tubes, had died. Their bloody remains lay in tatters along the after decks and guardrails. Another eleven had been wounded in various degrees and were under the care of the Surgeon-Lieutenant in the sick bay, in the officers' cabins and in the wardroom. The structural damage had been enough to force the destroyer to break off the picking up of survivors, now left to the gallant *Kipling*: immediately the bomb had hit, her rudder had jammed and she had become a menace rather than a help, and Sawbridge had taken her out of harm's way and then kept her zig-zagging, steering by the alternate use of his port and starboard engines. After superhuman work on the part of the shipwrights and engine-room ratings the rudder had been freed, and *Wharfedale* was once again under command. But both her after guns were out of action and would remain so short of a dockyard refit, while her stern plating and quarterdeck were badly damaged and there was much twisted metal around. The bombing attacks continued but by a miracle as it seemed – and by the sustained ack-ack fire from both ships – no more damage was done and *Kipling* remained totally unscathed throughout. At 1100 hours she signalled that she had picked up all survivors including Lord Louis and was pulling out. Immediately, Sawbridge made a signal asking permission to detach and take his damaged command back for the coast and the execution of his previous orders. The reply came back from *Kipling*: REQUEST GRANTED. THE BEST OF LUCK GO WITH YOU.

As *Kipling* turned away, she seemed to take the Stukas with her. *Wharfedale* lay doggo for a while longer, probably looking to the aircraft as though she was about to sink. When the attackers had passed out of sight, Sawbridge, by now somewhat adrift on his half-promised noon rendezvous, gave the orders for the return to Crete. Drummond said, 'Cameron won't be expecting us by the time we make the coast, sir. Not till after dark.'

'He'll be in the vicinity and on the lookout, Number One.' Sawbridge, capless and with his ginger hair blowing in a breeze, looked all around the horizons through binoculars. 'The sooner we get him away the better. No point in marking time, is there?'

Drummond nodded. 'I suppose not, sir.' He added, 'We're damn lucky the propellers didn't get twisted up.'

'You can say that again, Number One.' They were in fact moving at full speed again and would be off Sphakia in little more than an hour. As Sawbridge had said, the sooner they were away again from Crete, the better: no time currently to see to the dead. They would have to be committed to the sea once they were away and bound back for Malta. Sawbridge grieved for his dead: it wasn't only Lord Louis who knew his men personally. Commanding Officers of destroyers were closer to their ratings than were the captains of the capital ships and cruisers. Sawbridge detested the letters that had to be written to parents and wives: each one left its mark on him.

The war was getting filthier; the machine-gunning of the men swimming for their lives had left Sawbridge feeling murderous. He looked up now at the empty sky, clear blue and sun-filled, and wondered when the next attack would come. If the troops from the north were assembling at Sphakia and Tymbaki they were probably getting the brunt of it. Sawbridge sent up a prayer of thankfulness that he wasn't a soldier; at least a ship had speed and could twist and turn as the bombs came down.

It was a little after 1330 hours when *Wharfedale* reached the position off the coast where Cameron had left the ship the night before. Sawbridge and Drummond, with the Officer of the Watch, scanned the coastline through binoculars but found no sign of waiting men. Nor was there any signal. There was a strange silence, the quiet before the storm perhaps. Sawbridge had half expected to find the whole area ablaze. Perhaps the southward movement of the shattered armies hadn't yet started after all.

Drummond asked, 'Do we wait around, sir?'

'I'll give him a little longer, Number One. Just a little longer.'

Drummond said no more. He understood his Captain's thoughts well enough. No one liked the prospect of pulling out and leaving men behind; but Cameron had known the score and Drummond believed he would have holed up somewhere once the noon rendezvous had passed and would simply wait for the ship to come back in after dark. Meanwhile, a curious sense of unease began to grip the ship's company. The coast was too quiet; it couldn't last. It was almost as though they had been lured into some sort of trap. And every moment they lingered off Crete increased the danger. The proper place for a ship was out in the deep sea, with plenty of room for manoeuvre. The Stukas were not likely to be found well out to sea in any case; their best targets were the land forces and any ships they happened to spot in the inshore waters.

7

WHEN that scream had come, they had all stopped dead. Kopoulos said, 'That is the girl.' His voice was flat, dead-sounding. Cameron saw the movement of his hand but was too late to stop him; the knife, drawn down from the German officer's neck, was thrust into the back, angled for the heart. He dropped without a sound. Kopoulos gave the body a kick as it lay on the ground. The Greek's face was contorted, devilish. He said, 'The Nazi lied. Razakis is in his cave. The sound came to us from an air-shaft. Come.'

He turned back into the circle of rocks, moving fast. Cameron and the rest followed. Kopoulos led the way into a narrow passage leading off the central area, running deep between the rocks, and then from this into another passage, even narrower, with only just room for a man to squeeze through. Farther along it widened out a little and ended in a curious round stone of immense size; it must have been delicately balanced for when Kopoulos gave it a gentle push it swung aside. Beneath it a hole gaped blackly. Kopoulos said, 'There are steps. Feel carefully for them. When you are inside, it will be safe to use the light.'

'Right,' Cameron said. He was aware by now of his flesh wound, but the bleeding had stopped. He passed the word back for the signalman to hand the battery Aldis along. Kopoulos went down through the hole. Cameron had a word with Pike, whom he was leaving in charge up top, giving his orders and stressing that a full alertness would be needed. 'There may be other German troops in the area,' he said.

'Watch out for any signs of them. All right, Petty Officer Pike?'

'All right, sir.'

Cameron turned away and went down the hole in the wake of Kopoulos. Flicking on the Aldis he saw that the steps, cut out from the solid rock, were short, and led straight into a low but sizeable cavern where he had to bend almost double to avoid hitting his head on the roof. A middle-aged man lay on a pile of sacking, his face haggard. Like Kopoulos, who was now bending over another figure on a pile of sacking, this man was heavily built, and bearded. Razakis . . . Cameron was about to identify himself when there was another long-drawn scream from the second pile of sacking. Kopoulos moved aside, shaking his head, and Cameron saw the girl, Razakis's daughter. She was little more than seventeen or eighteen, he fancied, and she had once been pretty. Now, her face was ravaged by pain; she tossed and turned on the rough bedding and seemed to be sweating profusely, and was talking to herself in a high, monotonous voice. Cameron saw that Kopoulos was shaking like a leaf himself; perhaps there had been something between him and this girl notwithstanding the difference in their ages, and his dedication to Razakis was not all party loyalty. Kopoulos spoke to Razakis in his own language, briefly, then turned to Cameron.

He said, 'This is Razakis. I have told him who you are and why you have come.'

Razakis said, 'Welcome.' He reached out a hand; Cameron went forward and took it. The grip was firm, though the Greek looked ill and weary. Razakis spoke in English. 'Forgive me if I remain lying down. I have little strength left.'

'Your daughter,' Cameron said. 'What is the matter with her, Razakis?'

Razakis seemed to have difficulty in answering at first. Then he said in a shaking voice, 'It was the Nazis. They wanted information from me . . . I would not give it. They used my daughter Alexia to try to make me talk. They inoculated tetanus into her, and left us alone here so that I might watch her suffering, and then talk to prevent a similar thing happening to me.'

Cameron caught his breath, deeply shocked and horrified. He glanced at Kopoulos. The Greek's face was working and tears were visible; the hands clenched and unclenched as though in spasm. Another scream came, wrenching at Cameron's heart, at his nerves. How Razakis could have borne this . . . he asked, 'Did you talk, Razakis? You could not be blamed—'

'I did not talk!' The man's eyes blazed with anger. 'Never would I talk to the Nazis!'

'I apologize,' Cameron said. He was sweating now; the atmosphere in the cave was close, but it wasn't that alone. He was wondering what was now to be done, how to handle Razakis. This was no straightforward job of bringing out a man and a woman and getting them to the coast for pick-up. The girl was clearly in no fit state to be moved, and Razakis himself was far from well and would have to be carried. But there were other matters as well: if Razakis had things to tell, it was desirable that he should tell them now. It might be difficult to persuade him; he looked the sort who trusted no one and would prefer to keep information to himself until he could deliver it in person . . . but deliver it to whom, and why?

Cameron said, 'Orestis Kopoulos has told you who I am and that I have been sent to take you aboard a British destroyer—'

'You have been sent by Winston Churchill?'

Cameron smiled. 'I have been sent by my Captain, acting under orders deriving from Winston Churchill. Do you trust me, Razakis?'

'I trust Orestis Kopoulos, and I believe he trusts you. In any case, you are well vouched for by him, and I know both he and you speak the truth about your destroyer.'

'Then perhaps you'll tell me what it was the Nazis wanted to know?'

Razakis frowned. His teeth showed between stretched lips as more sounds of agony came from the girl; he seemed to

69

be bearing the pain as well as his daughter, the pain that Cameron knew would come with every movement, with every sound to strike her ears. Razakis said, 'This I cannot do. Until I am out of Crete I must not speak.'

'But if you should fall into German hands again? It's not going to be easy to get you off the island. Also, there's going to be plenty of bombing along the coast as our troops move south. If you should die—'

'Yes. I understand what you say. But there is something else.'

'What else, Razakis?'

'I must stay where I am. My daughter Alexia must not be moved. I shall not leave her until she dies, as die she must. It is too late. Even a doctor could not save her now.'

Cameron was sweating more than ever. What Razakis had said was undoubtedly true; the process of dying had started already; there was no knowing when the end might come. And Razakis was clearly adamant. So was Kopoulos. Kopoulos, who had been listening intently to the conversation, came forward and put his hands on Cameron's shoulders, staring into his eyes. Veins were standing out like rope in his temples as he said, 'Razakis is to be left to do as he wishes, my friend. Neither you nor I will interfere.'

It was an *impasse*; Cameron had the feeling that even Winston Churchill in person would have made no progress against the Razakis–Kopoulos combination. Yet there had to be a way. He clenched his fists as once again the girl on the sacking screamed. He saw Kopoulos put his hands to his ears, his face contorting.

Up top, Petty Officer Pike had made his dispositions against any enemy attack; although the German troops below the Canea–Maleme road, referred to by the hussar major and notified to the landing-party by Sawbridge before they'd left the ship, were well clear of the strongpoint so far as was known, there could have been enemy movements subsequent to the last intelligence report. In any case, the lot that had been slaughtered – dropped in by parachute for their mission – could have had other units with them, men detailed for rounding up other partisans perhaps, and they might rendezvous back at Razakis's HQ; Mr Cameron, he'd been specific about an alert watch. Pike spread his men out, with orders to report immediately anything that was seen but not to open fire until told to do so by himself or Mr Cameron. And they were to keep hidden.

'Best defence,' Pike told them, 'is surprise. Let the buggers show themselves all unsuspecting like, *then* attack hand-to-hand.'

Every now and again Pike heard the screams coming from down below. It was a terrible sound that would drive them all round the bend before long. Pike dug his nails into his palms and swore aloud. Bloody Nazis! It had to be their doing. He walked round looking at the littered corpses, left where they had fallen, British and German together. Pike spent some while moving the dead seamen into more dignified positions and well clear of the Germans. It wasn't right, in his view, to leave them together with Nazis. And they would have to be decently buried, if possible, before the living moved out again, which Pike hoped fervently wouldn't be long. The best sight he would ever see in all his life would be the old *Wharfedale* lying off out at sea to pick them up. . . .

His sorting of the dead finished, Pike stood back and dusted his hands on the seat of his trousers. He'd done all he could for his shipmates and he felt better about them. He turned as he heard footsteps, and brought his revolver from its webbing holster, but it was only Cameron.

Cameron asked, 'Did you hear the screams?'

'Yes, sir, I did.'

'It's terrible down there.' Cameron was shaking badly, really upset, Pike thought. Cameron told Pike the full facts, and the petty officer was as shocked as he'd been himself. Pike looked again at the sprawled German bodies. Bastards. He'd have liked to have the chance of killing them all over again. Cameron was going on, 'Every time anyone speaks, she

71

suffers. I had to get out. Kopoulos and Razakis are keeping quiet, not talking.'

'Is there nothing we can do, sir?' Pike asked.

'I'm afraid not. Other than shoot her like a dog. It would be better really. The end's going to come in any case ... but you can't do that.'

'No, sir.'

Cameron gave a strained laugh. 'Funny, isn't it ... you wouldn't let a dog or a horse suffer. Yet in a human being you just sit and watch.'

Pike said, 'Don't let it get on your mind, sir. It's happened before, in war. Not to say what *she's* suffering from, but something like. My sister ... she lived in London. She got it in the blitz last September. Trapped for hours, no one could get at her. Under a girder, she was. She screamed, they said.' Pike's voice shook.

'You were there?' Cameron asked.

'No, sir, but her kids were. Till someone fetched 'em away.'

'Oh, my God.'

'It's a rotten war, sir.' Pike's tone altered, leaving the past behind. 'This Razakis, sir. Do we know why it's so urgent he gets off to Greece, or where Winny comes in?'

'No,' Cameron said. 'No success in that direction. We've just got to get him away as soon as he's ready to go.' He meant, when the girl dies. He'd tried again to get some sense into Razakis, but he'd failed. The man was like stressed concrete. The girl's condition hadn't helped; each spoken word brought its reaction from her. Cameron had read about tetanus. Involuntary tonic muscular spasms, passing into paroxysmal convulsions. The inoculation of the disease could have been done any time from four to seven days earlier. The jaw was the first to be affected, then the face and neck. After that – not yet, in the girl's case – the trunk and limbs. Almost anything you cared to name brought on the intense pain – the smallest sound, a touch, a current of air, an attempt to swallow or move. The jaws would clench and the back arch. There would be a heavy rise in temperature, often to 105°

72

Fahrenheit. Even after death the temperature would remain, and even rise higher.

Cameron's reading hadn't informed him of when death might come. Meanwhile, time was short: there was the rendezvous to make. It could become necessary to use force; the landing-party had enough rifles to do just that, and there were enough of them left to disarm Kopoulos. Maybe.

Now the dawn was coming up; it was going to be a beautiful day, clear and bright once again, perfect weather for death to come like rain from the sky if the Stukas decided to come inland. The naval party was fully alert in its concealed positions behind the rocks, though there were yawns from tired men. And some muttering: the word had spread that the communist Razakis was being obstinate and was thus putting their lives in unnecessary danger. They were all worried now about that rendezvous; the *Wharfedale* wouldn't hang around indefinitely; no Captain would hazard his ship to that extent. If she went to sea, they might as well have joined the bloody Army – they would have to take their chances of evacuation along with the thousands of troops waiting to be taken off and that would be no joke. It would be like Dunkirk all over again: great columns of men, waiting for the orders of the beach-masters as the dive-bombers swooped. Waiting for the boats to be filled, waiting for them to move out to the ships, and return, and be filled again.

Not a healthy prospect. Blame began to be attached to the sub-lieutenant until Petty Officer Pike put a stopper on it. 'He's hamstrung, is Subby,' Pike said. 'He has to think of the girl.'

'I wish she'd stop bloody screaming.'

Pike said, 'So do I, but she's got it and we haven't. Just think about that, and shut your mouth.' He moved away, feeling a degree of disgust at the man who had spoken. He thought again about his sister in London, and the night he was devoutly thankful he'd missed. He thought about Devonport, too, and hoped his missus was all right. He saw the small house, now bombed flat, just off Fore Street that until a month or so earlier had run down to the main gate of the dockyard, and he saw Plymouth, and the Sound, and the First World War memorial to the men of the Devonport Port Division, on the Hoe where so long ago Sir Francis Drake had played bowls before drumming the Spaniards up the English Channel. *Drake he was a Devon man, and ruled the Devon seas* ... unconsciously, Pike began humming the tune, or something like it. Then, after a few bars, he broke off, looking surprised. From somewhere, another tune was coming. It didn't seem all that familiar at first, then he recognized it and it was 'Lili Marlene'. German basically, although the South African forces were beginning to pick it up. Pike didn't know if there were South African troops in Crete or not; but he wasn't taking any chances. He ran along the firing-step, alerting all the hands, then went down for the sub-lieutenant. He reported an apparent enemy advance from the north; maybe there had been another parachute drop, out of sight and hearing of Razakis's strongpoint.

'Any idea of their strength?' Cameron asked.

'No, sir. Fair-sized party at a guess.'

'And close.'

'Yes, sir.'

Cameron said, 'It's too late to evacuate. We'll hold the rocks, Petty Officer Pike.' He frowned. 'On the other hand ...'

'Yes, sir?'

'Razakis has to be got away. Those are the orders. That takes priority.'

Pike asked, 'A strategic retreat, sir?'

'Of a sort. I'll go below and put some dynamite up Razakis and Kopoulos, try to get them on the move and heading for the coast. I want you to hold the northern perimeter as long as you can. I'll take Leading-Seaman Wellington and leave the rest of the hands with you. I'd better take Lawrence,' he added, naming the signalman. 'Give me an hour's start, then move out behind me. All right?'

Pike said, 'Yes, sir. Just leave it to me.'

'When I make the coast, if the Captain's come back in, I'll get Razakis aboard then come back and wait for your party.' Cameron turned away and made for the narrow passage leading to the cave entrance. Then he turned again and called to Pike. 'Tell Wellington to report at once to the cave,' he said. He ran down the steps, flicking on the battery Aldis. The girl's screams had been continuing, heard above through the air channel, rising and falling, dying away for a while then starting again. Cameron sweated. As he entered the cave Razakis was staring at him; so was Kopoulos, who was still carrying the sub-machine-gun cradled in his arms. Kopoulos asked, 'Well?'

'There's a German force coming in, Kopoulos.' Briefly, Cameron gave the Greek the facts. 'We haven't more than a few minutes. We've got to move out.'

'No,' Razakis said. The voice was firm and determined.

Cameron said, 'I'm sorry, Razakis, but it's vital and I insist.'

'You insist! This is my business, not yours.'

'On the contrary. I have orders – orders, as you said yourself, that come from Mr Churchill. You're valuable to the Allies, Razakis. You must think of that – think of your duty. You've got not much more than a minute left.' Cameron turned his head as he heard footsteps coming down. A moment later Leading-Seaman Wellington appeared in the doorway, with his rifle in his hands. 'Stay right there, Wellington,' Cameron ordered.

'Aye, aye, sir.' Wellington, large and dour, seemed to take in the situation. He stood watchful, with his rifle ready, staring at Razakis and Kopoulos, his mouth a thin, hard line as he listened, so much closer now, to the girl's screams. Every time any of the men opened his mouth, it was going through her like a red-hot blade.

Razakis said, 'You talk of Churchill. He is a great man in his own country. Though his politics are not mine, I respect him as a leader and a fighter, and one who detests the Nazis as much as I. Yet my daughter comes first, Englishman. I wish –

75

yes – I wish to get back to Greece … but not without my daughter. I cannot leave her.'

Cameron nodded. 'I know. I understand, Razakis. But you have messages to deliver, things to report. You said so yourself. Tell me what the reports—'

'No.'

'Then tell Kopoulos!'

'It must remain in my head, Englishman!' Razakis's eyes shone in the light from the Aldis; there was an almost crazed look now. The situation seemed desperate; there was little time left and Razakis was adamant. Cameron turned and nodded to Leading-Seaman Wellington. Wellington brought up his rifle to cover Kopoulos; he drew back the bolt with a deliberate movement, slammed it back in, putting a cartridge up the spout. There he stayed, large and impassive, staring at the Greek. Kopoulos, who had been crouched beside Razakis, got slowly to his feet with his sub-machine-gun, his face working. If it came to a showdown, then Kopoulos had the clear advantage. Unless Cameron gave the order to Wellington in time … and yet Kopoulos was, by word of Winston Churchill, of Major Lumley-Gore as well, an ally, at least for current purposes *vis-à-vis* the situation here in Crete and in Greece.

Cameron was about to give the order for Wellington to drop Kopoulos, and the Greek seemed about to speak, when the sound of rifle fire came from above.

Now it looked like being too late.

8

PIKE had sent a man down to report: the Germans had come in openly, obviously expecting a friendly reception. The naval party had picked off three of the leading files as they had come out of the hills to the north and started the climb up to the strongpoint. The rest had immediately scattered to the rear, back into cover, and currently there was a lull in the firing.

It was Kopoulos himself who unexpectedly resolved the situation in the cave. He lowered his sub-machine-gun and some of the tension went out of the atmosphere right away. He spoke to Razakis in his own language, quietly, insistently, going down on his knees and taking the man's shoulders in his grip. All Cameron could do was wait; he gestured Wellington to lower his rifle. The girl on the sacking was writhing and contorting, the spine arching backwards as the medical books had said. Torture was there before Cameron's eyes, remote-controlled, postponed agony implanted by the Nazis. Hate filled Cameron's mind, similar to the hate of the two Greek communists. After some three minutes, long minutes that seemed like hours to the waiting men, Kopoulos got to his feet and faced Cameron.

'He will leave,' he said. 'Razakis is a patriot, and he will leave. I have put his clear duty to him.'

'And his daughter?'

Kopoulos didn't answer right away. He looked across at the tortured form, by now almost unrecognizable as a young and pretty girl, and he shook his head. He said simply, 'Razakis knows his duty. I shall say no more. Now we shall leave quickly, and make south for the coast. You will go up, please, with Razakis and your seaman.' He bent and lifted Razakis; Cameron went forward and gave a hand. Razakis was heavy, and was stumbling about; the march to the coast was likely to take a good deal longer than the two hours it had taken them to come north. At the foot of the steps Kopoulos handed over to Wellington; Razakis turned and looked at his daughter, tears brimming over to roll down into his greying beard. He didn't approach her; probably, Cameron thought, he realized it was too late now and all he could do would be to torment her further.

Razakis turned away again; Cameron and Wellington helped him, with difficulty, up the steps and along the narrow rock passage at the top. Pike came down at the rush from the firing-step.

'The buggers are still in cover, sir. I reckon they were mighty surprised at what met them. They'll come out soon, though, likely enough.'

Cameron nodded. 'Well, they're giving us a start, anyway – that's if we can get away without being spotted. Keep them busy when they do start, all right?'

Pike grinned. 'I'll do that, sir, don't worry!'

'Then I'll see you on the beach.'

'Aye, aye, sir. Sure you don't want more hands, sir?'

'You'll need them more than me.'

'I wouldn't be too sure of that if I was you, sir. You don't know what you're marching into.'

'That's a chance I'll take. Good luck, Petty Officer Pike.' Cameron shook Pike warmly by the hand, only too conscious that he was leaving the PO and the others to possible death or capture. He felt he was pulling out to safety himself, and never mind the only-too-likely hazards of the southerly march; but Razakis was the vital one among them all and he it was who had been charged with the personal responsibility.

Pike said, 'Best of luck to you too, sir,' and saluted smartly. He gave a sigh as the officer turned away, with Razakis being supported along by Wellington and Signalman Lawrence. It was a nasty old job, Pike reckoned, for a newly-commissioned youngster of little more than twenty. The lad had guts ... a moment later Pike stiffened and looked about him: firing had come again, but it wasn't the bloody Jerries this time.

It had come from below.

Cameron heard it too; so did Razakis. Razakis seemed to clench his whole body like an enormous fist, then he relaxed and gave a sob. They had been passing the air channel; the sound of firing had been loud and clear. Cameron, his own eyes moist now, urged Razakis on. From the narrow rock passage Kopoulos came out, his eyes wild, his face gaunt and grim, and the sub-machine-gun still giving off smoke.

He joined the others without a word.

Cameron couldn't get it out of his mind as his party moved as fast as possible down the slope and into the trees. The girl had been going to die anyway and the best possible thing had been done; there could be no doubt at all about that. If Pike should fail to hold the Germans off, her end would have been terrible to think of.

It was nonetheless tragic; but it was a part of war as war had developed. There was no room for decency now; all that had long since gone and he who was chivalrous lost out, could lose the war by humane instincts. It was the Nazis who had begun it, the Nazis who had dragged the world down with their own unholy baseness. Hitler's men; not the old German Army, most of whose personnel, Cameron believed, detested the orders they were forced to obey. Thus the onward march of progress, a hideous progress in which the good became bad and the bad became worse in a universal attempt to survive.

Razakis had no backward looks towards the strongpoint. He moved along painfully but doggedly, half carried through the trees over the rough ground, behind Kopoulos who was once again acting as guide. As they had moved away, the sound of firing had come again from their rear; Pike was in action, holding the Germans back. And now, as they went farther south, they could hear aircraft, zooming over them and heading, like themselves, for the coast.

Cameron said, 'It sounds as though the troop movement may have started.'

'Maybe, sir. If it has, I just hope they bloody make it out of Sphakia,' Wellington said with feeling. 'It must be bloody murder up there in Suda Bay, and I've got a brother in the Leicesters. He was in Greece ... now I reckon he may be up there, that's if he got out of Greece.'

A little awkwardly Cameron said, 'Well, here's wishing him all the luck in the world, Wellington.'

'Thank you, sir. That goes for me too if I need to say it.' They pushed on. After a while Razakis was forced to halt for a while and rest. He was panting like a steam-engine and his face beneath the hairs of the beard was sick-looking, with an unhealthy colour. Kopoulos came to squat by his side, looking anxious himself, shaking his head sadly. Kopoulos was still suffering terrible remorse for what he had had to do to the girl; Cameron fancied that would remain with him for the rest of his life.

Wellington looked at his wrist-watch. 'Just after ten, sir,' he said gloomily.

'I know.' Two hours to go to the rendezvous; they had not made all that much progress so far. It was touch and go. Cameron doubted if the Captain would keep the ship on station for long after the noon rendezvous had passed. And a whole day's wait could be fatal if the Stukas were attacking.

A head showed incautiously and Pike took quick aim with a rifle and fired. The head vanished.

· 'Don't know if I got the sod or not,' Pike said. Like Leading-Seaman Wellington farther south, he looked at his watch. 'Another half an hour, Martin, and we'll shift out. Strewth, I'll be glad to see the ruddy hogwash again!'

'Me too,' Able-Seaman Martin said, squinting along the sights of his rifle and watching out for another head to show. Bloody Nazis ... Martin, a three-badgeman and too old, he thought, for this shore-side lark, lived in Plymouth like Pike. Not far from Pike, in fact, before the blitz; close enough for their families to have shared a bomb if they'd been unlucky. Even as the thought came to him, Martin surreptitiously shifted his hands on his rifle and crossed his fingers, then patted the stock of his rifle, three times, touching wood. If anything should happen to Doris and the children ... Martin had a daughter, like that Razakis had had; just fourteen she was. What might happen if the Germans ever landed in Plymouth didn't bear thinking about. Martin felt a wave of cold fury sweep over him whenever he thought about that girl down below in the cave, now dead. But this was Crete, and therefore different; maybe the Huns got their ideas from wild, savage men, which the Cretans were by all accounts. They would be more civilized in Guz, perhaps. It was still horrible to imagine them goose-stepping along where Fore Street had been, though, and over the Hoe – bringing their bloody landing-craft into the Cattewater and their bigger ships past the Hamoaze and Devil's Point, coming ashore in the dockyard with their Nazi armbands and all.

Pike, too, was thinking about that silent body below. He said suddenly, 'That cave, Stripey.'

'Yes?'

'When the Jerries take over, after we've pulled out ... they'll go down there, right?'

Martin nodded. 'I s'pose so, yes.'

'Doesn't seem right, doesn't seem decent. Look, the Jerries are quiet now. We've got the grenades ... get down there, will you, Stripey? Blow in the entrance. Seal it off far as you can. Like a – a—'

'Shrine?' Martin suggested, wiping a hand across his nose.

Pike nodded. 'That's right, yes. A shrine, like. Least we can do, eh?'

Martin went down; Pike stared across at the hills and the trees. Beautiful, if you were a tourist. Pike liked mountain country, but not just at this moment. Crete was anything but a tourist spot and God alone knew what slaughter was going on along the coasts ... as he ruminated, the explosions came from below him. There was a lot of acrid smoke and German heads appeared again. The rifles fired, and they ducked down. Pike grinned; those explosions would be causing a certain amount of bafflement in the German minds down there. He heard Martin coming back up and he glanced down.

'Well?'

'All okay,' Martin reported. 'That revolving stone went ... split in two, and I reckon it's blocked the steps good an' proper. *And* I brought down a lot of the passageway leading to it.'

'Good work, Stripey.' Pike looked at his watch again. 'Fifteen minutes more, then we'll give the buggers a farewell round or two, and after that—'

'We scarper!'

'Right.'

Pike fancied they would have a fair start; the Jerries wouldn't come out from cover too fast after the firing stopped. They'd smell a trap – bound to. Once into the trees, the landing-party would have a good chance of getting clear away to the coast, just as good a chance as Cameron in fact. Pike whistled flatly through his teeth. It was hot now, with the sun well up the sky, and the sky a metallic blue, acting as a reflector almost. The Germans were being remarkably quiet, Pike thought with a sense of sudden unease, very strangely quiet. He moved away from Martin and walked round the firing step, having a word with each of the seamen, warning them that in the next few minutes he would fire two rounds rapid with his revolver, this being the signal for them all to blast away towards the concealed Jerries, twelve rounds each. After that, no time lost at all, they were to beat it down the slope to the south and re-muster in the cover of the trees. Pike was going back to his command position when he heard a yell from Able-Seaman Martin:

'Christ, the sods are coming in!'

Coming round the rock, Pike saw them. Around a couple of hundred of them at a guess, and more were coming from the flanks. Pike shouted for the rifles to open. Some of the running men went down sprawling, but far too few of them. Martin fell backwards with a bullet in his head, and plummeted to the rock surface below. Two of the ratings broke to the south, leaping like stags down the slope. They had very nearly made the trees when the machine-guns got them. Three bullets took Pike in the chest as he pumped away with his revolver; his last thought before he died had been about that letter home. It was still aboard the ship. The fighting was all over inside the next five minutes. Twice within a few hours Razakis's stronghold had lost its defenders to a man.

1415 hours: it was time to go now, to lie off well to seaward before the Stukas came back, and then return after nightfall. Sawbridge, his heart heavy, passed the orders.

'Full ahead both engines, starboard ten, Pilot.'

The navigating officer spoke down the voice-pipe; Sawbridge could hear the Torpedo-Coxswain's voice coming back up as he repeated the orders: 'Full ahead both engines, sir. Ten of starboard wheel on, sir.' Then a moment later, as bells rang below: 'Engines repeated full ahead, sir.'

'Steady,' Sawbridge said fifteen seconds later, watching the gyro repeater.

'Steady, sir. Course, one-eight-oh, sir.'

Sawbridge nodded to the navigator. 'Steer that, Pilot.' He moved for'ard and looked down to the fo'c'sle. He called, 'Number One?'

Drummond looked up, shading his eyes against the high sun. 'Sir?'

'We'll remain closed up at first degree of readiness, Number One.'

'Aye, aye, sir.' Drummond walked aft. Dinner, already eaten, had been brought to all hands at their action stations; tea and supper would be the same. The men were getting tired now; their reactions would be slower when action came again. They were bored, too, and Drummond was far from prised. Mostly, action itself was of short duration, however hectic while it lasted. Hanging around at action stations when not in actual action *was* boring – very. And continual action stations was unbeloved of the Executive Officer of any warship large or small; routine work just didn't get done and after a while the ship began to look and feel dirty, like a neglected house. Paintwork went for a burton. When possible, First Lieutenants of destroyers and Commanders of cruisers and battleships liked to enter harbour looking spick and span with paintwork gleaming; it was akin to the Brigade of Guards marching off the little ships after Dunkirk – *marching*, not shuffling, with polished boots. Bloody stupid in a sense, but excellent for morale.

Drummond moved around the decks, having a word here and there, helping so far as he could to keep spirits up and keep the men on their toes. He knew very well how all hands hated air attack, from the dive-bombers especially. It was a mode of warfare that left men livid with sheer fury at the way the Stukas screamed in and after the bombs had gone at once screamed out again, allowing virtually no time for the guns to hit back. It was like being snapped and snarled at by terriers, fast-moving and vicious. Surface action was different: the enemy stayed there to be shot back at. Or anyway, the Germans did; in Cunningham's Pond, the Italians usually didn't.

Kopoulos had handed his sub-machine-gun over to Cameron and then Razakis had been lifted on to his back to be carried. Kopoulos was strong, but Razakis was immensely heavy; thus the advance south had slowed considerably and at a little after noon, with some way still to go to the coast, Kopoulos had stopped and lain Razakis gently on the ground.

'He is very, very sick,' Kopoulos said. 'The rough going is not good, even when he is carried. It is his heart.'

'Is he likely to have a heart attack, then?' Cameron asked.

Kopoulos shrugged. 'Me, I am not a doctor. I do not know,

84

but to go on would make it likely, perhaps. You see his colour.'

'Yes,' Cameron said. Razakis's face was now almost purple; he had to rest, that was obvious. Cameron seethed with impatience and frustration: the *Wharfedale* would – or rather, might – now be lying off for the pick-up and she wouldn't wait beyond the rendezvous time, or not long anyway. Cameron asked Kopoulos how much farther they had to go.

'A little more than four miles,' Kopoulos answered.

'Then we can't possibly make it. On the other hand, if the ship waits a while, one fit man might make it on his own and send a signal asking my Captain to wait—'

'Perhaps,' Kopoulos said. 'But that man would have to be me, since I alone know the track. And I shall not leave Razakis.'

'But look—'

'No, my friend, I am adamant.' Kopoulos reached out a hand for his sub-machine-gun, which Cameron had laid on the ground beside him. Re-armed and determined, the Greek went on, 'Out in the open, if your destroyer has gone, there is danger. We know the destroyer will come back tonight. Therefore we must wait for night, and the rest will be good for Razakis.'

Cameron had no option but to agree; and Kopoulos was probably right at that. In the meantime, they were all hungry. Iron rations had been brought from the ship and Razakis and Kopoulos had brought with them an apparently inexhaustible supply of goat's-milk cheese, which was nourishing enough. They had a makeshift lunch in the trees, and, from a canvas bag belonging to Razakis and dangling from Kopoulos's shoulder, the Greek brought a bottle of local wine. This he passed around as they munched cheese; it was white and vinegary, with a foul taste, but at least it was liquid. Cameron grew sleepy, but fought the feeling off by getting to his feet and walking about. Kopoulos, seeing the difficulty the Englishman had in keeping his eyelids open, made a suggestion.

'We shall use the time for sleep,' he said. 'We shall take watches. We must be sensible. Tired men become useless. We have a lot of time to spare until dark, my friend.' He ran his fingers through his beard. 'I shall take the first watch.'

Cameron was glad enough to sleep. Kopoulos sat with his back against a tree, his mouth full of cheese and the sub-machine-gun laid across his knees. Prudently, he left the rest of the bottle untouched. Wellington and Lawrence also slept; Razakis lay inert with his eyes open and his chest heaving, until at last he closed his eyes and slept like the others. They were all left to sleep on until they woke of their own accord. Cameron was the first to wake. It was still broad daylight; his watch now showed 1535 hours.

'Your turn, Kopoulos,' he said.

Kopoulos shook his head. 'I do not find sleep easily, my friend, and I do not need it as other men need it. I shall remain awake.'

Cameron fancied that the death of Alexia Razakis was the cause of the man's wakefulness; his conscience wouldn't give him respite, though his act had been one of sheer mercy. Kopoulos seemed to want to talk, though not of the girl. He began speaking of Greece and of what the Germans had done and were doing there, of the horror of the Nazi advance that had ejected the Allied armies. As he had mentioned before, he had himself been tortured by the Germans; after his escape, his immediate family had suffered, all of them: his wife and two sons had been shot by firing squads, his brother and sister-in-law had died under the brutalities of interroga-tion, his parents, both of them in their seventies, had been dragged from their beds and beaten to death with rifle-butts. All known communists in Greece were at similar risk. As for Razakis, although he had never been taken by the Germans whilst in Greece, his family had suffered also; he had had four more children, two sons and two daughters beside Alexia, and all had died at Nazi hands.

'Razakis is a hero,' Kopoulos said. 'To go back again to

Greece ... it is crazy, but heroic.'

'And you, Kopoulos?'

'I shall not go back to Greece. I have work to do here, on behalf of Razakis. I shall take his place as the leader of the partisans in Crete.'

'You're not coming aboard my ship, then?'

Kopoulos shook his head. 'I shall see Razakis safely aboard, and then I shall go.'

'Go where?'

Kopoulos laughed harshly and said, 'Somewhere, my friend! It is better that no one knows where I go next, for then there can be nothing given away – I do not suggest that you would do so, but if matters should go wrong, as so often they do ... then no one knows better than I the methods used by the Nazis to extract information. Do you understand?'

'Yes, I understand, Kopoulos.' Cameron hesitated. 'I've said this before but I'm saying it again: wouldn't it be wiser for us both to know what Razakis has to report – in case, as you've said, things go wrong and Razakis dies?'

'No,' Kopoulos said flatly. 'I do not care to repeat myself. I have spoken of torture. Each man has his breaking-point. I know mine. I do not know yours.'

'You don't trust me?'

Kopoulos said, 'It is not a question of trust, Englishman!'

'I think it is. You seem certain of your own breaking-point, and—'

'I have been tested. I did not talk.'

'No. And all honour to you. But what makes you think I would?'

Kopoulos laughed and said, 'Pink-and-white faces, unlined faces ... faces without beards ... no, they have not the experience of life and death that comes to aid a man when under interrogation. It is hard to explain, but it is something I feel here.' Kopoulos laid a hairy-backed hand over his heart. 'By no means do I accuse you of possible cowardice, you must understand that. But the Nazis are animals, and—'

Suddenly, Kopoulos broke off. With an astonishingly swift

movement of his arms, he brought up the sub-machine-gun and fired a short burst into the trees to his right. Cameron had seen nothing; but as the echoes of the gunfire died, a man crashed into view, falling with his right shoulder shattered. A German steel helmet rolled from his head as he fell. Kopoulos squirmed his body to lie protectingly in front of Razakis, and swung his gun in an arc, his eyes searching the trees.

9

THERE was a dead silence. Wellington and Lawrence were watchful behind their rifles; Razakis seemed almost to have stopped breathing. Then Kopoulos got up and moved at a crouching run towards the German, who hadn't moved but was staring back at the party of apparent partisans, wide-eyed and fearful. Cameron got to his feet and joined Kopoulos.

'See,' Kopoulos said. 'As well as the shoulder, he is hit in the leg also. Now we must find out more.' He bent and took the man by the collar and dragged him unceremoniously towards the group around Razakis. The German whimpered with pain and fear; he was just a youth, Cameron saw, a year or two younger than himself he thought. Kopoulos asked him, roughly, if he spoke English.

'*Ja*,' the soldier answered. His face was dead white and the lips trembled.

'Good,' Kopoulos said. 'You will now talk. Where have you come from, Nazi?'

'From Vitsilokoumos.'

'North of Sphakia ... the road from Canea and Suda to Sphakia! Your armies are there, Nazi?'

'*Ja, ja* ... yes.' There was no holding back on the young German's part. 'We were fighting the Australians, and there were tanks.' Tears were running down the face now. 'I ... I ran away. I am not a Nazi ... and I was frightened.'

'Not a Nazi, but a coward.' Kopoulos spat full at the young man; the gob dribbled down the face. 'I do not like cowards.

89

Now, come, tell me more things. What was happening in your sector, around Vitsilokoumos? Tell me, and do not lie.'

'The British were coming down the road from Canea. That is all I know.'

Cameron caught Kopoulos's eye. He said, 'That must mean the withdrawal from Suda, Kopoulos. It's begun.'

'Yes. And the coast near Sphakia will be saturated by the Nazi dive-bombers. It is not good for us – for Razakis.' Kopoulos turned back to the German. 'If there is more to tell, tell it. If you do not, I shall shoot your other shoulder, after that your other leg. You will live, Nazi, to die in much pain.'

The agonized voice said hoarsely, 'There is no more to tell. I swear that. I am – was – just a soldier, a private. I was confused by the noise, by the gunfire, by the screams of men. I knew only that my unit was moving south towards Vitsilokoumos, from Askifou—'

'And your unit, Nazi?'

'No. 100 Mountain Regiment, of the 5th Mountain Division under General Ringel.'

'And you . . . you were the only one to desert, to run away?'

'I – I don't know. I believe so. No one came with me. I am alone. I am at your mercy. I surrender. For me, the war is over, and I am glad. I am not a Nazi, only a private soldier.' The man was sweating with pain and fear now, and still tearful. Kopoulos walked a little way off, frowning, and beckoned to Cameron.

He said, 'The Nazi has told what he knows. There is no more to come. If there was, he would tell it. What he has said is useful. Do you know what I think?'

'Go on, Kopoulos.'

'I think that what you were saying earlier was perhaps right.'

'You mean—'

'I mean this: there are Germans in the vicinity . . . there is obvious danger, now that the southward thrust of the British has started and has drawn the Nazis with it. Both you and I

90

should know what is in the mind of Razakis. I will have words with Razakis.'

He moved away.

It took time; Razakis was obstinacy personified. Kopoulos, however, was persuasive and persistent. Razakis, he said, was sick and might die; his words must not die with him. Razakis answered that he would not die until his mission for Winston Churchill was complete; he would keep going and it was vital that he should reach the Greek mainland as quickly as possible. Kopoulos pointed to the wounded German, telling Razakis that the Nazis were close and were advancing on Sphakia. There would be difficulty in bringing in the destroyer safely, and even after he was aboard, if he got aboard at all, the dive-bombers would give the ship no peace. He might be killed; and before that could happen, he might be taken by the Nazis and that would be the end. The repetition, the persistence, the quiet firmness penetrated at last. Razakis spoke. He had received orders, he said, from Mr Churchill via a high-ranking officer of British Military Intelligence: there had been rumours of recent weeks that all was not well with the German–Russian alliance, that misconceived marriage of opposites that Razakis had never been able to accept in his mind. These rumblings were, of course, known to the Allied governments, and the intelligence services had been probing further, with interesting results: in Greece had been a certain highly-placed German, a close confidant of the Führer himself. This German was understood to be suffering severe disillusionment with the vision-inspired strategy of Adolf Hitler, and his Party loyalties were said to be under strain, largely on account of the very fact that Hitler was bent upon turning against Russia. If Hitler should commit his armies and aircraft to an assault on the huge Russian land mass, then, this VIP believed, Germany would lose the war. The German's precise whereabouts were not known to the British, but word had been passed to Razakis, then in Greece himself. The partisans' grapevine went into action and the German had been located. Orders had come for his kidnap so that he could be made to talk about his Führer's plans in regard to Russia. Razakis had organized the kidnap and brought it off successfully while the British forces were being evacuated from Greece under ferocious German attack following upon the thrust of the Führer's armies down from the Yugoslav border and the Aliakmon Line.

Willingly enough, the German had talked: Herr Hitler was indeed about to send his armies, his infantry and artillery and armoured columns, and his air power, into Russia. His objective was Moscow itself, and on the way he would devastate the Russian countryside and smash the cities.

Cameron asked, 'When is this to be?'

Razakis said, 'On 22 June. The code name is to be Operation Barbarossa. It will open along many hundreds of miles with a massive artillery barrage. Hitler expects to take Brest-Litovsk within two days, and by that time to have totally destroyed the air power of the Soviets.'

'And Russia ... do you mean to say, Razakis, that no rumour of this has reached Moscow and the Kremlin?' Cameron was incredulous. 'That you alone—'

'I do not say that, Englishman. But Comrade Stalin does not, will not, believe that the Nazis are about to turn against him and to abrogate the treaty. Nothing has made him believe, but now he will believe. You understand?'

'Not quite,' Cameron answered. 'Are you saying he'll believe you, Razakis, when he hasn't believed anyone so far?'

Razakis said quietly, 'He will not believe unless I am put back on the mainland of Greece to be joined by the German, who is currently in the hands of my partisans on the island of Kithnos. At the last moment, when I was brought out to Crete, matters went astray. It was not possible then to embark the German from Kithnos, and by the time I knew this I had already left myself, and the boat would not turn back. Now I must go back, and take the German across many frontiers into Russia, to tell his story to Comrade Stalin in person.' He paused, and stared hard at Cameron. 'In the meantime your part, if I should die under the German attack here, must be to inform Winston Churchill of what I have found out. It may not be enough ... Comrade Stalin may believe it to be a British trick, if Churchill should inform him. It remains vital for me to go back to Greece to collect the German, whose words will convince.'

They remained where they were until the sun was well down, then they got on the move again, carrying the wounded German with them while once again Kopoulos took Razakis on his broad back. For some while now they had listened to the sounds of bombing coming up from the south, and Cameron was fearful of what the *Wharfedale* might be undergoing as she moved back in for the rendezvous. As they came to the high coastal rock and looked down towards the beach, they could see, away to their right, the fires flickering over the port of Sphakia and could hear the explosions as the bombs dropped.

There was no sign of the *Wharfedale*; the time was a little after 1930 hours – half an hour to go yet. No point in worrying, Cameron told himself, Sawbridge wasn't likely to come in early; the shorter the period he had to cruise off-shore, the safer. The party remained on the heights, watchful and silent. Cameron thought about Petty Officer Pike and the others back in the rock stronghold. When after an hour or so of the southward march Pike hadn't shown up, Cameron had not been too worried. There was catching-up to do. But as time had passed and no one had come, the likely facts had had to be faced. There could be no going back to look; Razakis was still his first concern. But Cameron had finally given the word to march on again with a heavy heart. It felt like a desertion. War looked worse than ever.

He stared out to sea, fancying that he saw a ship's outline now and again, but one that he was unable to hold. As yet there was no moon, no stars; there was some overcast that should be a protection to ships at sea, but it was making vision difficult. Wellington said, 'Just on 2000 hours, sir. Use the Aldis, sir?'

'No. There's time yet. I wasn't to flash till I'd seen the ship.'

'Captain's a punctual officer, sir. Always has been.'

'I'm not worrying yet, Wellington.'

'No, sir.' Wellington fell silent. The German soldier was whimpering again, as he had whimpered and cried out at intervals during the march; the sound, like that made by Razakis's daughter, rasped at the nerves. Cameron half wished he'd left the man behind. But he hadn't been able to bring himself to do so and never mind the strictures of Kopoulos, who clearly regarded him as soft-headed. Enemy or not, the man would get medical attention as soon as they were aboard . . . but where in hell was the *Wharfedale*? On the bottom already? What Leading-Seaman Wellington had left unsaid nagged at Cameron as they went on waiting for something to show out at sea: unpunctuality, at any rate in Wellington's mind, meant that something must have gone wrong. 2015 came and went and still no sign. Cameron risked the Aldis and found it had packed up. At 2035 they heard the dive-bombers scream down, two of them, to send their bombs on to the water just offshore. They were ready for them, lying flat on their stomachs in the crevices of the rock. The din of the twin explosions was tremendous, and there was a good deal of flame. Still no ship visible: what were the Jerries doing, wasting their bomb-loads?

'Don't usually drop on sod-all,' Wellington said. 'Know something, sir? I reckon the buggers are out for us, and—' He broke off as more Stukas came in; this time the bombs dropped closer, and shingle and rock fell around. Some of the rock put the German soldier out of his misery. A chunk smashed his head, and the whimpering stopped finally. 'See what I mean, Mr Cameron?' Wellington asked.

'We'll move back,' Cameron said. They did so, fast. As they flattened once again, more attacks came. It did look as though they were expected. Cameron didn't believe that any of Pike's party would have talked, but as Kopoulos had said earlier, every man had his breaking-point. Assuming they hadn't talked, the incoming Germans could have put two and two together: Razakis gone, and the British Navy holding the strongpoint. It wouldn't be too difficult to make an assessment and come up with the right answer. He should have thought of that....

This was the time for decision. Cameron got to his feet. He said, 'There's only one thing to do. Sphakia's in British hands still or they wouldn't be bombing it. We'll head in for Sphakia and get ourselves a boat. Then we'll go to sea and hope to be picked up.'

Kopoulos said, 'We can make for Greece if we find a boat.'

'No.' Cameron was firm. 'We head for my ship. I have to get Razakis's message transmitted urgently to Alexandria – to Admiral Cunningham—'

'There will be someone with a wireless in Sphakia, Englishman.'

'Perhaps. We'll see. In any case, it'll have to be encyphered first. One more thing, Kopoulos: from now on this is my show. You've done your part and I'm more than grateful. Now it's up to me to get us off the best way I find. If I can get a boat, you're free to leave us as you said you intended.'

Kopoulos didn't answer, but bent his back ready to take Razakis, and within a minute they were on the move again, heading west along the high ground for Sphakia. Behind them, the Stukas continued their relentless attack on the empty beach. *Wharfedale* was hardly likely to come in now; she would most probably turn back if she was making her approach, and get well to sea. Or – again he thought of the worst – she had already come under attack, as they would themselves just as soon as they entered the port. It was going to be a hazardous business to say the least.

Within an hour, after a hard slog along the heights, they were approaching Sphakia, or what was left of it. The entry was difficult and must have been sheer hell for weary troops; there was no road closer to Sphakia than a couple of miles and the journey ended in a 500-foot descent via goat-track down a cliff. As they scrambled down to the bottom and came into the shattered port in which not a building seemed to have been left, the racket was deafening, terrifying. Fires blazed everywhere as the bombs fell and the Stukas screamed in to blast the little shingle beach into oblivion and render it useless for an evacuation. There were troops everywhere, masses of them, all the various units mixed up in a great, unwieldy conglomeration of sweat-streaked, bloodied men. British, Australians, New Zealanders ... gunners, infantry, armoured columns, signals, engineers, RASC bereft of their trucks. Officers and NCOs were bawling out orders but the dispirited troops seemed to be taking little notice as they huddled in such cover as they could find and waited for the Navy to come in and take them off to the ships. As Cameron's party moved along in the light from the fires and the bomb bursts, their way was blocked by a sergeant of the Leicesters, brandishing a revolver.

'What are you lot?' he demanded, looking all set to shoot.

Cameron said, 'Royal Navy, Sergeant. Special mission.'

'Navy my arse.'

Leading-Seaman Wellington moved forward and said, 'The officer's right, Sergeant. And my name's Wellington. I've a brother in your lot, don't know if you know him, eh?'

'Wellington?' The sergeant stared back at him quizzically. 'Duke Wellington ... yes, I knew him. Come to think of it, you look like him an' all. He'd just been made a lance-jack,' he added.

Wellington asked, 'Why the past tense, Sergeant?' His face was suddenly set into harder lines, visible in the light of the fires.

'Sorry, mate.' The sergeant put a hand on Wellington's shoulder. 'He bought it, up north. Took four Jerries with him. Guts ... he'll likely get a gong.'

'You can stuff the gong,' Wellington said harshly. He turned away. Then he looked round again and said, 'I'm glad to hear he got four of the bastards, though.'

96

The sergeant nodded and turned to Cameron. 'Anything I can do, sir?'

'I want a boat,' Cameron said. 'I have to rejoin my ship. I suppose you've no news of the *Wharfedale*, by any chance?'

'Never heard of her. There's a rumour four destroyers are coming in – *Napier*, *Nizam*, *Kelvin* and *Kandahar*, but I don't know for sure. Anyway, they'll only take off about a couple of thousand men at most.' The sergeant pointed. 'If you want a boat, the port's down there, if you call it a port that is. Shingle beach, twenty yards by a hundred and fifty ... that's our assembly point when we get the orders to go.'

'Thanks. I'll get along there.'

'Best o' luck, sir.' The sergeant gave a hurried, sketchy salute and dived for cover as a Stuka screamed down. The bomb hit little more than fifty yards off, and more debris rose to drop back in dust and broken rock. Cameron moved his party on towards the beach, expecting at every moment to be blown to shreds. Some good providence was protecting them, it seemed; all around troops were lying dead or shockingly wounded, and detached parts of bodies were in evidence everywhere. Sphakia was becoming little more than a charnel house and if this went on much longer the destroyers would have nothing left to pick up – but then, no doubt, more and more troops would be coming in, a never-ending stream of them in the terrible retreat from Suda and Canea.

Wharfedale had made her approach a little late. It was 2015 hours when Sawbridge stopped engines off shore and tried to pick up the coastline through his binoculars. So far he was keeping well out, but would close the moment he saw Cameron's Aldis flashing for pick-up.

'No sign,' he said after a long look. 'Number One?'

'Nothing, sir,' Drummond said.

'He may be there or he may not. I'm not risking making a signal.' Sawbridge waved a hand towards the clear signs of the attack on Sphakia. 'Those buggers'd be on us like a ton of bricks. Cameron should be able to use his Aldis from the cliff crevices, though.' He took another long look. 'Still nothing. I'll take her in closer, Number One. This rotten bloody visibility isn't helping. It's not helping us, it's not helping Cameron.'

'It's not helping the Germans either, sir.'

Sawbridge grinned. 'True. It's an ill wind! We mustn't complain, I suppose.' He went to the gyro repeater. 'Engines slow ahead,' he ordered down the voice-pipe. 'Starboard five.'

The destroyer moved in, ghosting along through the overcast, moving slow so as not to bring up a bow-wave that might give away her position. Sawbridge watched the shore, closely and carefully. Still no signal. He swore, his nerves on edge. Once again he stopped engines and lay off, drifting until the way came off the ship.

He said, 'I don't like it, Number One. Cameron's had all day to get here.'

'He should be all right assuming he made it to the stronghold in the first place – his track south won't have been anywhere near the line of retreat from Suda, and it's there the German attack will have been concentrated.'

Sawbridge nodded, then said, 'I'm beginning to wonder if he ever got to Razakis.' He looked at the time: it was 2035 hours. At that moment, the bridge personnel heard the shift in the racket from the diving Stukas. It was coming their way now. As the sighting reports came in from the lookouts, Sawbridge passed the inevitable orders.

'Engines to full ahead, port fifteen. Steady her on one-eight-oh, Pilot. We're getting out.' He had scarcely finished speaking when the first of the bomb bursts took the beach, and shingle and water erupted. One after the other, pounding and blasting . . . if Cameron was arriving after all, he certainly wouldn't be lingering on that beach. Already Sawbridge was starting to frame the signal that would have to go to Admiral Cunningham in Alexandria: it would be brief enough in all conscience – mission unsuccessful. But Sawbridge had a feeling it wouldn't end there. Razakis had sounded somewhat more than important, though God knew why. Frankly, however, Sawbridge was not too much concerned about Razakis.

His ship's company was more important in his eyes. Inside the next few minutes, he had something else to worry about. He had evidently been spotted by the Stuka pilots, and in they came, vicious as ever, spitting out bombs.

Once again, Sawbridge turned and twisted his ship this way and that, unpredictably, as his close-range weapons did their best to send their bullets through the perspex windshields into the pilots' brains.

10

THE search for a boat was a hopeless one: Cameron had never expected Sphakia to be as bad as he had found it, and neither had Razakis nor Kopoulos. There was nothing left that floated, and if there had been then the troops would have found it first and used it to get away from slaughter. But according to Kopoulos, there was a tiny bay a little to the west of Sphakia, towards Cape Krio. It was unlikely that it had been found by the troops; there was no way of approaching it other than from seaward. Also, it would almost certainly be free of the Stukas.

'How do we get there?' Cameron asked.

'We swim,' Kopoulos said.

'With Razakis?'

'I shall take him. I am a good swimmer. It can be done.'

'And there'll be a boat?'

Kopoulos shrugged. 'Perhaps, perhaps not. But undoubtedly there is none here! It is very possible that some fishing boats will have fled from Sphakia, and taken refuge in the bay.'

'Right,' Cameron said. 'We'll give it a try. Anything's better than this!' He led the way down the shingle. Kopoulos passed his sub-machine-gun to Razakis to carry and, if possible, keep clear of the water. He was much attached to the weapon.

'She is my good friend,' he said. 'Where I go, she also goes.' Supporting Razakis, he waded in deep, then turned over on his back and, holding Razakis by the shoulders, thrust out strongly with his powerful legs. The naval party entered the water behind Kopoulos and followed him towards the west.

The swim was not in fact very far; as they came round a small headland and left the aerial attack behind them, they saw a small patch of shingle beach ahead and to their right, standing out white against the sea through the continuing overcast. Within a few minutes they were safe ashore, wading up the shingle. Already they had seen no less than three fishing boats hauled up on the beach, their Cretan crews standing by them and watching the fires of Sphakia lighting the skies eastward of the headland.

As the party came ashore, one of the fishermen approached with his rifle aimed. There was a shout from Kopoulos, and the man lowered his rifle but remained looking watchful and anxious. Lowering Razakis gently to the pebbles, Kopoulos spoke to the man in his own language and then turned to Cameron.

'All is well,' he said. 'This man is a patriot. You may have his fishing boat. He would like it to be returned if possible, but if it is not possible, then I have told him that Winston Churchill will provide him with another as soon as the war is won.'

Kopoulos stood with a hand at the salute and his other hand clutching the sub-machine-gun as Cameron took the fishing boat out into the night. Once again Cameron had offered to take the Greek off with him, but it had been no more than a formality since he realized Kopoulos had made up his mind and would stay to be a thorn in the side of the Germans once they had occupied the war-torn island. Cameron was sorry to part; Kopoulos had been a good friend and without him nothing at all could have been achieved. Before they had left, Kopoulos had kissed Razakis on both cheeks, hugging him close. Then a firm handshake all round and that had been all. Cameron watched as the hand came down from the salute and Kopoulos strode back up the beach and vanished in the darkness. He wasn't risking going back to Sphakia, evidently; although he had said there was no way of approaching the bay from landward, he obviously knew of some precarious goat-track that he would be able to negotiate but which would be unknown and inaccessible to British soldiers.

With the sail set, a light breeze carried them well offshore. Cameron made his course south-east, towards where he expected the *Wharfedale* might be cruising if she were still afloat. As he went, he thought about the fishing boat's owner; Winston Churchill might never know, might never pick it up amidst all the details of a world war, but Cameron had signed a dirty piece of paper produced by the Cretan, who had scribbled on it in some sort of patois. Kopoulos had laughed heartily but passed it; Cameron had no idea of what he had committed the British Government to, but it had been a case of needs must.

They sailed all that night over a dead calm sea, moving at last away from the fearful battle over Sphakia, not coming under any attack themselves and finding no vessels of any kind. But as a splendid dawn came up to dapple the eastern sky with brilliant colours, the low silhouette of a warship came up ahead. Cameron maintained his course and somewhat precariously climbed the boat's mast for a better look. As they closed, Leading-Seaman Wellington called from the stern, 'It's her all right, sir! It's the old *Wharfedale*.'

It was like a first-class hotel by comparison with things past; after making his detailed report to the Captain, Cameron was sent down for a bath while Sawbridge questioned Razakis. When the questioning was finished, Razakis was taken to the sick bay and handed over to the Surgeon-Lieutenant. Cameron, clean and in uniform again, was sent for to join Sawbridge on the compass platform.

Sawbridge said, 'I've sent a cyphered message asking for orders, Sub. About Razakis. Do we take him to Greece, or is he required in Alex? If the matter's as vital as he says, I'll get my orders pretty fast, I imagine.'

'Yes, sir.' Cameron paused. 'And his message, sir, about Russia ... are you transmitting that?'

'No,' Sawbridge answered. 'In my view it's too lethal, as it were, to risk being broken if the Germans happen to have our current recyphering tables – I have to consider that as a possibility. What I intend to do is to close the main Fleet units off Scarpanto and pass the message by hand of officer to the Admiral in the *Queen Elizabeth*. I fancy he may detach a destroyer for home – a fast boat could reach Portsmouth in three days, and secrecy's more important even than speed.'

'A hand message for the War Cabinet, sir?'

Sawbridge nodded. 'Right! It's bloody cumbersome, but that message is dynamite. Just so long as the German High Command remains unaware that we have the information, it could give Russia time to prepare and give Hitler a nasty shock!'

'Razakis made the point, sir—'

'Yes, I know all about that – he has to get that German VIP into Russia, personally. Well, I'll have my orders as to that shortly.' Sawbridge scanned the sky and the horizons all round his ship, which was steaming eastwards at full power. There was no sign of any enemy; once again, it was like a peacetime cruise. But in the Eastern Mediterranean peace could go very suddenly and all hands knew it. There was no lack of vigilance as the seamen lookouts watched their arcs and the guns' crews stood ready for instant action.

Below in the petty officers' mess there was talk amongst those off watch – talk about Pike. Pike was badly missed; he'd been a cheery messmate, one of the best there was. And it was rotten bad luck to go and buy it ashore and to be left to rot in a dump like Crete. Soon, as in the case of all the others who had died, there would be a messdeck auction of his personal gear, an auction at which his mates would bid extravagant sums for things of no real worth; the proceeds would be handed in due course to his widow in Devonport ... if ever they saw Guz again, that was. The Torpedo-Gunner's Mate was already having a preliminary sort through Pike's possessions and now he found the letter, addressed to Mrs Pike. The TGM tapped it thoughtfully against Pike's locker, shaking his head sadly. Post it when they got back to base, or forget it? You never knew with letters, or with women either. Something could upset Mrs Pike. On the other hand, he'd written it meaning it to be read ... well, it could wait anyway. Probably he *would* post it.

He spoke later to the Torpedo-Gunner, but not about the letter. He said, 'It must have been a rotten job, sir. *Bloody* rotten.'

'It's a wonder,' Vibart said, 'that any of 'em ever got back at all. I reckon young Cameron did a good job, eh?'

'Pity he lost Pikey.'

The Torpedo-Gunner poked a finger forward. 'Now look here, Charlie, he didn't lose Pike and you know it. He was carrying out his orders, and Pike died as a result. And it looks like the mission was successful, right? We've got that Razakis to prove it.'

Something similar was said in the wardroom when Cameron went down to snatch some breakfast. Congratulations were offered; Cameron said it was all due to Orestis Kopoulos, and he meant it. Also, he said, it was far from finished yet; they might be ordered to put Razakis ashore in Greece. Probably would be, seeing that they had him aboard and were handily placed to alter towards the mainland.

They were.

The orders came promptly, just as Cameron had finished eating, and were decyphered with all the speed demanded by the Most Immediate prefix: Sawbridge was ordered firstly to close the battleship *Queen Elizabeth* south of Scarpanto, and then to detach at full speed for the Aegean.

The big ships were around 150 sea miles to the east-north-east of *Wharfedale*'s current position; by 0900 hours the destroyer was off Kufonisi and altering a little northward. At a few minutes after 1000 hours she raised the great hulls of the heavy ships – the battleships *Queen Elizabeth* and *Barham* and the aircraft-carrier *Formidable*, all ready to bombard Scarpanto. *Wharfedale* identified herself by flashing her pennant numbers and was ordered to close. As she swept up towards the heavy squadron, the *Queen Elizabeth*, wearing the flag of Vice-Admiral Pridham-Wippell, began flashing from her signal bridge high above the water.

Wharfedale's Yeoman of Signals reported: '*Wharfedale* from the Flag, sir. Do not propose stopping engines owing to likelihood of attack from Scarpanto. You are to encypher your message and pass groups to me by light.'

Sawbridge grinned; he had already prepared for that, and Razakis's message was all ready to go, brief and to the point. In plain language it read: GREEK PARTISAN RAZAKIS KNOWN TO CHURCHILL REPORTS GERMANY TO INVADE SOVIET UNION 22 JUNE.

It would be something of a bombshell.

The message was passed by light and acknowledged. On its heels Sawbridge sent a signal of his own: FLAG FROM WHARFEDALE, PROPOSE TO PROCEED IN EXECUTION OF PREVIOUS ORDERS.

The moment this was acknowledged, Sawbridge began to draw away from the Fleet units, laying off a course north-westward to take his ship through the strait between Plaka and Kaso Island into the Aegean. The great battleships reared far above the destroyer's decks, immense above their anti-torpedo bulges, the superstructure rising hugely over the fifteen-inch guns in their massive turrets already elevating to begin the bombardment from almost ten miles' range. Cameron, standing on the compass platform as they moved past, looked back at the battleships with something approaching awe. They were magnificent if already dated; great leviathans fast becoming as extinct as the brontosaurus, slow and unwieldy in action, too vulnerable to that new concept of war, the dive-bombing attack in force. But they were still splendid and impressive, still the repository of ultra-smartness and discipline, brimming over with gunners' mates, still carrying some of the old titles that were no longer relevant to the rest of the Navy: Captain of the Fleet, Master of the Fleet ... titles redolent of Nelson and all the years between. Cameron wished them luck in their action against Scarpanto and its air bases, hoped fervently that good providence would protect them and their vast ships' companies when the Stukas struck; and then turned away from them as they began to fade into the waters behind. He had a different war to fight as he headed with Razakis into the Aegean.

Razakis seemed a little better; even a few short hours in a comfortable sick-bay cot had made a difference – that, and nourishing food. Pills provided by the doctor would take their effect in due course. The Surgeon-Lieutenant reported to Sawbridge and Cameron that the partisan leader was in not too bad a shape basically but really needed a much longer rest than he looked like getting. Razakis, notwithstanding the fact that his captured German VIP was being held by the partisans on the island of Kithnos, was far from anxious to be landed in Kithnos himself; he might not be able to reach the mainland from there, and it was the mainland he was aiming for, had been aiming for all along. Sawbridge, whose orders had stipulated no particular landing place, considered he had *carte blanche* to direct his course as events might dictate. After talking to Razakis again, it was in his mind to make a landing on Kithnos, find the German and bring him aboard, and then head well north with both the German and Razakis. Speed was vital to Razakis, and it was obvious that the closer to Russia he could be landed, the more chance he would have of evading the Germans, and the faster would be his journey to Moscow.

In the meantime, Razakis was a source of wonder to the ship's company; word about his daughter had spread, so had word of involvement at a high level, involvement of the Prime Minister himself, no less. *Wharfedale* looked like being right in on the making of history, though what that history might be no one apart from Razakis himself, the Captain, and Cameron, yet knew. Rumours abounded along the messdecks as the destroyer passed through the straits and entered the danger zone to the north of Crete, her plates vibrating to the tremendous thrust of her propellers under full power.

'Probably gold,' an able-seaman suggested darkly. 'Them Greeks, they're stuffed with it. Winnie's going to nick the lot and flog it to the Yanks ...'

'Could be a plot to assassinate some sod. Hitler, Goebbels, Himmler ...'

'All the way from bleedin' Greece? Bull!'

'Think up something better, then.'

Round and round, and mouth to mouth; the ship seethed, and the tension grew. Distantly, before they passed out of earshot, they heard the tremendous roar of the broadsides from *Queen Elizabeth* and *Barham* as the bombardment began. Gunsmoke seemed to darken the horizon astern as the great fifteen-inch guns roared out again and again, sending their shells hurtling across the miles of sea. In *Wharfedale*'s own sector, the air was strangely quiet; no doubt the Stukas were too fully occupied with the bombardment of Scarpanto and the troops in Crete to bother with a single destroyer, but attack would come before long. The Germans wouldn't want a British warship penetrating the Aegean ...

During the afternoon watch, Sawbridge, after close study of the charts, went down with his navigating officer to talk to Razakis in the sick bay: he wanted to allow Razakis the maximum possible rest. He put his point about a Kithnos pick-up and an on-carrying to the north.

He said, 'Look, Razakis.' He spread out the chart and placed the tip of a pencil on it. 'I propose, subject to the course of events, to land you and this German *there*.' The pencil rested on the port of Alexandropolis in the far north of Greece. 'About four hundred miles from where we are now, maybe a little under that, but taking into account a deviation into Kithnos, four hundred's about right. Say, eleven to twelve hours' steaming, again disregarding Kithnos – we don't know how long we'll be delayed there, you see. From Alexandropolis you'll have to go through Turkey and reach the Black

107

Sea. Since we're bound to come under attack before long in any case, I'm prepared to break radio silence and request contact to be made with the Kremlin, asking for a pick-up at, let's say, Igneada in Turkey.' Sawbridge sat back. 'Now, how's that?'

Razakis was scowling. 'Me, I do not agree. I do not like the Turks. I shall not be landed in Turkey.'

'It's your best bet, Razakis.'

Razakis sat up in his cot. 'Not so. The Turks ... already they are half in the Nazi camp! There is the non-aggression pact with Bulgaria, and they did not interfere when Hitler's Nazis entered my country. The Turks are my enemies. Therefore I shall not land in Turkey, and that is my last word.'

Sawbridge said, 'You could be wrong about them being half in the Nazi camp, Razakis. I've seen intelligence reports that suggest they've put out feelers to us—'

'To the British? Yes, this also I have heard. The Turks are not to be trusted, and you British would be foolish to trust them.' Razakis brooded, scowling still. He went on, 'In any case, there is too much risk in your signal, Captain. I am a man accustomed to take risks, yes ... but in this there is too much, I think. Suppose the Nazis break your cypher? Then they or their tools the Bulgarians will be waiting off Igneada. There is another thing also, and it is this: Comrade Stalin will suspect a trap. He is, after all, at war with your country.'

'I take the point,' Sawbridge said, frowning. 'It's the same consideration you spoke of earlier, Razakis ... the Kremlin won't act on your message unless it's supported by your German friend. In which case, we're going to go round in circles!'

'Not I,' Razakis said. 'I shall go in a straight line! But not via Turkey.'

'Something like eight hundred miles from, say, Athens to the Soviet border ... hostile territory all the way, and the Bulgarian frontier to cross? Even if you get there at all, it's going to take the hell of a long time, isn't it?'

108

Razakis shook his head. 'Not so. There are many partisans in Greece and I shall have transport. In Bulgaria, too, I have many contacts.'

'Maybe, but—'

'You may leave that part to me, Captain. I can guarantee to be inside the Soviet Union within forty-eight hours of being landed, and that is quicker than if you were to offer to take me by sea all the way, even! All I ask of you is this, that you sail first to the port of Lavrion on the mainland, and then, when you have landed me, that you sail to Kithnos to pick up the German and bring him to me. It is on Kithnos that the Nazis will be expecting me, since the German is there – word of his presence may have reached the Nazis, you understand. They will not find him – but they will be on the watch for me.'

'And for us, too.'

Razakis shrugged. 'Perhaps. But I believe you understand. The matter is vital, and I must not be taken by the Nazis.'

Razakis must not be taken by the Nazis: that was true and was the nub of the whole operation. From it followed something more: Sawbridge had put it to Razakis that it would be best if he, Razakis, remained aboard the destroyer rather than be put ashore in Lavrion while the German was hooked away from Kithnos, after which they could both be landed together on the mainland; but Razakis had vetoed this. It seemed that he felt uneasy at sea and was loathe to have both himself and the German aboard the one ship at the same time. There might well be heavy attack on the *Wharfedale* off Kithnos, and if both he and the German were lost, so was the chance of convincing Russia of the Nazi threat. If one survived, the chance was there still. The German – Razakis had now revealed his name as Hermann von Rudsdorf, a highly-placed Party member in the German Foreign Ministry – could be taken into Russia by other partisans, and would be, if Razakis should be killed. When Sawbridge made the point that, once ashore, the two of them would be together all the rest of the way, Razakis said he was a landsman and a partisan and he knew how to remain safe.

As Sawbridge remarked later to Cameron, Razakis was determined to be awkward. 'He's an obstinate bastard, Sub!'

Cameron grinned. 'I've found that out already, sir.'

'Yes, I'm sure you have.' Sawbridge paused. 'Are you willing to try the German?'

'Sir?'

Sawbridge said, 'I expect to be off Lavrion by 2300 hours – I'm reducing speed so as to make a landfall in darkness. After that, Kithnos. I'm asking you to go ashore and bring von Rudsdorf off. All right, Sub?'

Cameron felt a sinking sensation in his guts; but he nodded and said, 'All right, sir, of course. What are the orders?'

'They're best given by Razakis rather than me! I gather he'll provide you with an authorization to his partisans and they'll cough up von Rudsdorf – they'll come back aboard with you in fact, acting as his escort. There's a bar where you'll make contact ... you'll need to have words with Razakis to finalize it all, of course, then you'll have to play it your own way.' Sawbridge lifted his glasses and examined the sea and sky. Nothing in sight; it was too good to be true and it couldn't last. They were right into the Aegean now, slap into broadly land-locked and hostile waters, Greece and its Nazi occupiers to one side, the enigma that was neutral Turkey to the other, a very nasty trap that could be closed behind them at any moment if the wavering Turks should finally throw in their lot with Hitler. Distantly to the north-east lay the passage of the Dardanelles; that offered a direct entry into the Black Sea and contact with the Russians ... it was quite a thought but it wasn't on. No ship, surely, could get through the Dardanelles and the Bosporous against the Turkish guns that would open upon any threat to their neutrality – and if it did, then it would be blown sky-high by the Russian fleet in the Black Sea, who would scarcely believe that one of His Majesty's destroyers could be steaming to their assistance. And in any case

110

Razakis wouldn't like it. Razakis, the landsman, wouldn't like it at all, and no more, probably, would his friend Winston Churchill if he was engaged in negotiations with the Turks...

The *Wharfedale* moved on, taking a wide sweep so as to avoid being sighted from the Kikladhes group of islands, steaming north through the Mirtoon Sea between Milos and the mainland. As the sun went down the sky, the peace – the peace that everyone aboard knew was very brittle indeed – stayed with the ship. Sawbridge, his nerves badly on edge as he went deeper into Greek waters, kept his ship's company at action stations. On the compass platform, at the guns and torpedo-tubes, there was a curious silence as the men waited for the shooting to start, the gunners in their anti-flash hoods and gloves looking like members of the Ku Klux Klan.

11

SAWBRIDGE'S ETA was dead accurate: at 2300 hours he stopped engines well to seaward and a little to the north-east of the small port of Lavrion, ghosting along in the starlit night until the way was off the ship and she lay motionless, no more than a shadow. From the compass platform the land was closely scanned through binoculars; it looked deserted. Sawbridge picked up the bay which Razakis had indicated on the chart as being his most likely landing place. Nothing moved in the bay so far as could be seen, and there were no ships, no boats of any sort, in the vicinity.

Again, too good to be true?

Sawbridge turned to Razakis, now out of the sick bay and standing beside him on the bridge. 'What do you make of it, Razakis?' he asked.

Razakis shrugged. 'There is as ever the risk. Without taking risks, I get nowhere.'

'You're a brave man.'

'No. I am a patriot. That is all.'

'You want me to put you ashore now?'

'Yes.'

Sawbridge sighed. 'Sooner you than me,' he said, and passed the order to his First Lieutenant to drop a Carley float in the water. Drummond was half-way down the ladder from the bridge when what looked like an inferno broke out from the shore. First, a searchlight was beamed towards them, then another and another, great shafts of light that swept the destroyer from stem to stern, illuminating her like day and revealing her for what she was. Immediately the shore guns went into action, heavy artillery that sent big shells winging out across the water; their rushing wind and whine could be heard and felt as they travelled over the *Wharfedale*'s decks and exploded beyond her to throw up enormous waterspouts. To her Captain's order, *Wharfedale* was already on the move and turning under full rudder for the open sea. Sawbridge, as his engines increased their thrust, zig-zagged between the shell bursts.

Razakis demanded furiously, 'Where are you going?'

'Out,' Sawbridge answered succinctly.

'But I am to be landed—'

'Over my dead body! I'm taking neither my ship nor you into that bombardment, Razakis, and you can shove that in your pipe and smoke it. What use would it be for you to land in the middle of all that?'

Razakis didn't answer, but turned his back and moved stiffly away to the other side of the bridge. Sawbridge, as the destroyer steamed fast beyond the range of the shore batteries without having been hit, pondered on the likelihoods raised by the sudden barrage. It seemed reasonable to suppose that they were being shelled simply as an enemy ship and not on account of Razakis. If the Nazis had known Razakis was coming in to land, then presumably they would have held their fire until he had done so and could be taken prisoner. They wouldn't want to scare him off. After a couple of minutes Razakis came back and said, 'I am sorry, Captain. I apologize.'

'It's all right, Razakis.'

'Of course I could not land in such a bombardment, and you were right. But there will be other places.'

'Not if all the Greek coast is garrisoned like Lavrion!'

'All the Greek coast will not be.'

'All the Greek coast *could* be, Razakis. To my mind, the risk's too great—'

'What, then, do you propose, Captain?'

Sawbridge said, 'I propose to pull out for Kithnos and

do my best to embark von Rudsdorf. After that – we'll see.'

'Does this mean that you still have Turkey in mind?'

'Maybe it does,' Sawbridge answered.

'I shall not land in Turkey!'

Sawbridge said, 'My ship goes where I say, Razakis, and you're in my hands.'

It was believed that already the German armies were starting to garrison the more important of the Greek islands; they might or might not regard Kithnos as worthy of a garrison, but Sawbridge assumed they would do so since Razakis had spoken of the Germans possibly knowing that von Rudsdorf was being held there. Cameron was faced with the trickiest of missions and he would have the best hope of success by going in alone. Razakis, since he had not after all been put ashore on the mainland, was loud in his insistence that he should go himself, but Sawbridge vetoed this.

'I'm responsible for you,' he said. 'You've already made the point, either you or von Rudsdorf has to live and get through to Russia. So you stay aboard.'

'That young man of yours . . . he has little hope without me.'

'That young man of mine,' Sawbridge said briskly, 'didn't do so badly ashore in Crete and you know it. And the original plan didn't envisage you being here at this stage anyway—'

'Yes, yes,' Razakis interrupted. 'Very well then, I must accept your orders. But if your Cameron fails to bring the German off, then he will face the anger of Winston Churchill himself, do you understand that?'

Sawbridge grinned at the words and the furious face of the Greek. 'I understand,' he said. 'I have every confidence in Cameron.'

In under an hour after the precipitate departure from the mainland, the destroyer was off the northern point of the island of Kithnos, once again lying with engines stopped and the way off the ship. Sawbridge was surprised that there had been no follow-up of the artillery bombardment; he had more

114

than half expected air attack, but that hadn't come, and he supposed that the Stukas were still too heavily engaged around Cretan waters to be spared over the mainland; and indeed the sea bombardment of Scarpanto by the British battleships, plus the air strike from the *Formidable*, might well have destroyed many of the Stukas on the ground. In the meantime Kithnos, like the mainland earlier, appeared quiet and peaceful, though with that earlier experience in mind no one was taking too much for granted. After a close scrutiny of the distant shore, Sawbridge nodded to Cameron, waiting on the bridge with his body darkened all over with black boot-polish and wearing only a blackened pair of shorts and canvas shoes.

'Off you go, Sub,' the Captain said. He held out his hand. 'The best of luck. I'll move farther out once you're away, and come back in four hours' time, remember.'

'Yes, sir.' It was a tight time-schedule, one that didn't allow of setbacks encountered *en route* for the hideout where von Rudsdorf was being held. The *Wharfedale* had to be away from Kithnos before the dawn and that was that; like the landing in Crete, Sawbridge would go to sea if Cameron failed to show, and return after the next nightfall if he hadn't been sunk in the meantime. Cameron went down the bridge ladder; a Carley float was already in the water awaiting him. With no delay he dived in cleanly, and came up right alongside the float. He heaved himself in and started paddling for the shore; as he moved away he heard the thrash of the screws as Sawbridge took the destroyer slowly astern, out again to sea. As he paddled, Cameron went again through the instructions given by Razakis: after he had landed, he was to follow a goat-track to a small village just under half a mile inland, due south of his landing point. There might be Germans around; if so, it would be up to him to keep clear of them. His goal was the first building he would come to on the outskirts – a bar run by a mainland Greek named Xarchios, who would be instantly identifiable by a deep scar running from below his left ear to the corner of his mouth, a scar upon which no hair would grow and which was wide enough to show clearly through the beard. To clinch the identification beyond doubt, Xarchios had a wooden peg-leg. He was a patriot, a partisan, a good friend to Razakis; he would lead Cameron to the hideout once he was in possession of the note from Razakis that Cameron carried wrapped in oiled silk in the pocket of his shorts, together with Razakis's written authorization to hand von Rudsdorf over. Cameron was not to enter the bar itself, for obvious reasons, but was to gain entry to the private rooms in rear and attract the attention of Xarchios. Xarchios, a much experienced guerrilla fighter and undercover man, would understand and wouldn't create any public disturbance over an intruder.

Nevertheless, it was a pretty tall order.

Cameron had asked what would be the result if he should be taken by the Germans and the notes read. Razakis had grinned and drawn a hand across his throat; and had added, 'But the letters . . . they must not be found or Xarchios will die. There are matches wrapped in the oilskin. The letters are to be burned in time, if you are in serious danger.'

That, too, was a tall order. An assessment would have to be made; he could destroy the letters too soon, and be left without authority, and then the partisans rather than the Nazis might do the killing unless he could talk fast and convincingly enough. His heart in his mouth, Cameron paddled on. He felt that the Carley float must stand out a mile beneath the moon and the stars: if only the weather had co-operated! When he was an estimated mile off the shore-line, he obeyed orders and went over into the sea, and, keeping his head below the gunwale of the float, swam and pushed onward. The theory was that if the float should be spotted it would be put down as being one from a sunken vessel drifting in on the slight onshore breeze and no more notice might be taken of it.

Might!

The theory was as full of holes as a sieve, in fact. The Germans were far from being fools, although according to Razakis they had rigid minds and the float's emptiness would

116

convey no more than the simple fact of emptiness. Razakis, in Cameron's view, tended, like Kopoulos, to underestimate the enemy, regarding them with a dangerous contempt. Cameron swam on; beneath his shorts, secured to his waist by a lanyard, a revolver wrapped in oilskin like the letters bumped uncomfortably yet with a faintly reassuring feel. At least he might take some Germans with him if the worst happened, as he felt by now convinced it must. However, in the event he landed easily enough and apparently unseen; the beach was deserted and he was soon in cover of the rocks with the Carley float drawn up on the shingle in the lee of a jutting overhang. He identified the goat-track as indicated by Razakis, and started the climb. It was not a long one. The track merged into a rough roadway, the one that would take him direct to the village; and within a few minutes of meeting this roadway he saw the small cluster of dwellings, standing out white beneath the moon. No lights were showing anywhere, and there were no people to be seen: the Germans customarily brought their curfew regulations with them. There were no German troops either, or if there were then they were keeping hidden. Cameron was moving fast now, hugging the lee of the rough, crumbling wall that ran alongside the road. As he closed the village outskirts, he saw a light and caught the sound of music and singing, and laughter. This was coming from the bar run by Xarchios; curfew or no curfew, the Kithnos Greeks were not kept from their liquor. Razakis had said, if they couldn't leave the bar because of the curfew, then they would remain there through the night.

Cameron halted, keeping close to the wall. Cautiously, he looked over. There was a rough, rock-strewn field, with a solitary goat tethered to a wooden post. Again following Razakis's instructions, Cameron got quickly over the wall, paused a while until he was sure no one was about, then ran, bent double in the lee of scrubby bushes, across the field diagonally to his right to come up at the back of the bar.

Then he became aware of the Germans. They were in good cover and could be seen only as dull gleams of moonlight on the metal of their steel helmets. They made no apparent movement: possibly he had not been seen, or more probably, he thought, they were waiting for him to show his intentions by approaching the bar. And if that was so, then the involvement of Xarchios in the capture of von Rudsdorf must presumably have become known to, or at any rate suspected by, the German authorities, who were now waiting to put the bar owner into the bag. After that, von Rudsdorf himself. It was clear enough now to Cameron why the Germans hadn't been watching the coast. Why bother, when all they had to do was to hang about at the goal-post and then make their arrest?

Cameron had flattened to the ground on sighting the metallic gleams and currently lay hidden behind a large boulder. Now there was a waiting game to be played out: one side or the other – assuming Cameron had been spotted – had to make a move. Cameron grinned tightly to himself; it wasn't going to be him, even though he had a schedule to keep to and if he missed it, the *Wharfedale* would go to sea without him. She would come back in. If, now, he moved towards Xarchios's bar, he would be either dead or in the bag to face execution as a spy, unless the Germans were willing to accept his blackened Naval shorts as an item of service uniform.

He believed he had been seen. The helmets moved, the outline of the German uniforms came into view, so did the muzzles of their rifles, which were most likely the 7.99-mm KAR-98K carrying a five-round magazine. The sentries seemed to be conferring, seemed to be uncertain, possibly wondering whether or not they had been seen by the intruder. Then their doubts appeared to be resolved: they moved out from cover, two men with some dozen yards between them, coming fast for where they had last seen Cameron, moving at a crouching run with their rifles ready. Behind his boulder Cameron had his revolver out, and now he thumbed back the hammer. He might not have much of a hope of coming out of this, but at least he might get one of the German soldiers. From his cover he chose one of them, the man on his right, and waited for him to come within revolver range. Then, suddenly and just at the wrong moment, the silver light dimmed as a large cloud rolled across the moon. Cameron lost sight of the man he had been watching and when he picked him up again, both he and his companion had moved on past him; neither of them could have been more than a matter of yards from him to each flank. Now they were still moving at their crouching run, pursuing nothing with dogged Germanic determination.

Cameron grinned again and lost no time. Getting to his feet, he ran lightly towards the back of Xarchios's bar and a gate into a small walled garden. The Germans were quite oblivious. In the garden's safety he paused to take a breath, listening to the sounds of revelry coming from within, then he approached the back door. It was unlocked; he lifted the catch and went in. He entered a short passage, lit by a flickering oil lamp. Light was coming from round the jamb of a door at the end – light and noise: the bar, obviously. Remembering Razakis's instruction not to enter the bar, Cameron opened another door, one to his right, took a step forward into darkness, and then plunged painfully on his back down a flight of stone steps, crashing at the bottom into something hard. There was an almighty crash and bottles broke around him; he seemed to have overturned a bottle-rack. He got up, felt himself for broken bones and other damage, and found that he was intact though undoubtedly badly bruised.

Light shone down from above and in its glow Cameron saw a wooden peg-leg. Clearly, he had now attracted the attention of Xarchios. As the man came down the steps cursing angrily the light showed the bearded face and the wide, hairless scar. Xarchios began asking questions in his own language. Cameron answered in English. 'I come from Razakis, who is aboard a British destroyer. He sends these.'

He handed over the oilskin-wrapped letters. Xarchios gave him a long, slow look, then read. Having read, he nodded and said, in English now, 'The letters are genuine, this I know. I was expecting Razakis himself.'

'My Captain decided it was better he didn't come.'

'So you were sent, yes. And you want the German. You were not seen to come? The sentries—'

'They're looking for someone they won't find.' Briefly, Cameron explained. He had just finished when there was a heavy banging on the back door and then the sound of it being flung back on its hinges. Xarchios turned away and went fast up the stone steps, carrying his lamp. There was a loud conversation, a hectoring one on the part of the returned sentries, who seemed to be insisting on a search of the premises. There was a language difficulty; the soldiers spoke no Greek, Xarchios had no German. They reached a compromise on English, of which the Germans had a smattering. Cameron listened.

Xarchios was saying, 'Oh, yes, now I understand. Yes, there is an intruder ... a man who has entered my cellar and smashed bottles.'

'We go,' a German voice said.

Xarchios said blandly, 'You know where the door is.'

'To the cellar, fool!'

'By all means.' In the lamp's light, Cameron saw the Greek stand aside, smiling obsequiously. His heart like lead at an apparent betrayal, Cameron felt around for his revolver, which had clattered away when he fell; he couldn't find it. He was aware of the Germans moving towards the top of the steps, was aware of Xarchios putting his lamp down on the floor of the passage and then moving up behind the two men ... and then, very suddenly, the soldiers crashed down the steps, bouncing and pouring blood. Hardly a sound had been uttered. Cameron, dodging the bodies, saw Xarchios, now with his lamp in his hand again, coming down the steps, smiling and happy. Cameron looked again at the bodies: each had landed face down, and from each back a knife-haft protruded. Xarchios said, 'A double thrust ... my left hand is as strong as my right, and with as true an aim for the heart. There will be no trouble until the guard changes. By that time, we shall be with von Rudsdorf.'

'And after that, Xarchios?'

'After that – to the beach, my friend!'

Cameron said, 'I meant what happens to you when the Germans find the bodies?'

'There would be much trouble, for I cannot dispose of the bodies in time. Von Rudsdorf comes first. This place will be no longer safe for me, for Xarchios, and I have no family left now ... I shall come with you to your ship.'

Von Rudsdorf was not far away from the village, which was fortunate: time was running out fast. Xarchios, who was armed with a sub-machine-gun, was unworried about the curfew; it was a risk, certainly, but one that had to be taken if the German was to be got away. 'The Germans are not yet fully organized,' he said as they made their way into the countryside from the rear of the bar premises. 'They are not strong in Kithnos – they need all possible forces on the mainland and in Crete. We shall not be seen.'

Cameron asked, 'Can we make it back to the beach before dawn?'

'Yes.'

Xarchios was running now, fast for a heavy man; Cameron had difficulty in keeping up with him. Shipboard life didn't make for fitness in marathon runs. After some ten minutes, the Greek slowed. The moon's light was streaming down again now, and as the two closed a hillside Cameron saw the dark shadow that indicated the entry to a cave. Xarchios advanced towards this entry at a trot, carrying his sub-machine-gun loosely in one hand. It was Cameron who spotted the glint of the moon on metal, just inside the cave entrance. He gave a warning, but Xarchios laughed and said, 'It is my friends, who guard von Rudsdorf.'

He began to shout a greeting; but before he had uttered more than a word or two the cave entry came alive with flame and smoke as the concealed guns opened fire.

12

XARCHIOS fell to the ground, cursing and holding his left upper arm. He dropped the sub-machine-gun. As the German bullets zipped around, ricocheting off the rock, Cameron flattened beside the Greek.

'Take my gun,' Xarchios said.

Cameron did so. As the Germans showed themselves by their gun-flashes, he fired a long burst. There was a cry from the cave mouth, and the German guns stopped firing. Cameron, breathing hard, asked, 'Now what do we do, Xarchios?'

'There is another entry,' Xarchios said. His arm was pouring blood now. 'The Germans may know of it, and they may not. It would be better for us to use it, rather than advance into more gunfire, perhaps.'

'Is it far?'

Xarchios gave a laugh that ended in a wince of pain. 'There speaks the British officer who is worried about his deadline! Von Rudsdorf comes first, the deadline is unimportant . . . but no, it is not far, though it means a hard climb. Come – but remain flat on the ground.'

The Greek squirmed away to the rear. Cameron followed on his stomach, feeling the stickiness of Xarchios's blood on the hard ground. There was no more firing from the cave entry; it seemed that any further German troops were awaiting the next move from the intruders rather than stick their necks out again; but soon there could well be a reconnaissance party sent out to investigate. Xarchios meanwhile was moving fast. Once again, Cameron had a hard job to keep up; within minutes his unprotected body was torn and bruised from the crawl over the rocky ground as he followed the partisan leader around a great jagged outcrop to their left – a welcome enough shelter, temporarily at any rate, from the Nazi guns. Once past the outcrop, the climb began. Xarchios remained on his stomach; the moon was too bright for risks to be taken now, and the clitter – the age-old volcanic rubble – gave adequate cover if care was used.

The climb was sheer hell.

Up and up, crawling painfully. Cameron's knees and elbows suffered the most, but his entire chest and stomach seemed to become raw meat as the climb continued without respite and, seemingly, without end, right up to the heavens and the unkind light of the moon. From below them now, there came the sounds of men on the move. They heard voices; these spurred Xarchios on to superhuman efforts of speed. The Greek was bleeding still, losing, Cameron thought, far too much blood to go on for much longer. The breathing of both men became painful and gasping. But at last the ordeal came to its end, and Xarchios slowed, then stopped and put out a hand to Cameron.

'Ahead and to the right,' he said. 'Do you see?'

Cameron looked towards the bearing as indicated. 'See what?' he asked.

'A hole. A hole in the ground . . . what you in England call a pothole, I believe. Come!' Xarchios moved on again, once more halted Cameron as he approached the pothole. Now Cameron could see it: a hole, perhaps three feet across, obscured until now by thickly-growing scrub. Xarchios said, 'My arm. The blood pours too much. You know how to apply a strip of shirt so that it stops the flow?'

'I'll manage,' Cameron said. He helped Xarchios to pull off his shirt and then ripped a sleeve from it, found a suitable piece of dead wood from a bush and twisted the shirt-sleeve above the wound. Xarchios thanked him and then the two men pulled themselves to the lip of the hole: it yawned black and dangerous, dropping into the earth's belly, a terrifying pit. Xarchios said, 'It is easier than it looks.'

'You've been down it?'

'Many, many times. The tunnel slopes, at first steeply, then more gently, and the sides are smooth.' The Greek paused. 'I cannot promise what may be at the bottom. There may be Nazis. But now we must take the risk if we are to get von Rudsdorf out of Kithnos. You are willing?'

Cameron nodded; he had no option. Orders were orders, and his were clear enough. Xarchios said, 'Good! I shall go first. You will give me fifteen seconds, then you will follow. You understand? Fifteen seconds for safe clearance, no more, no less.'

'Right,' Cameron said. He studied his wrist-watch, took his time from the moment Xarchios went over and vanished at speed into the hillside's depths. Fifteen seconds precisely ... then, taking a deep breath and offering up heartfelt prayers, he swung his legs into the hole and let go of the surface. It might have been an exhilarating sensation in other circumstances but not now. The descent was appalling: he seemed to drop like a stone, drop into the totally unknown at high speed, hardly touching the sides at all until the steep incline eased and the speed came off gradually. Now the front of his body was in full contact with the tunnel; Xarchios had been right – it was astonishingly smooth and hard, like glass.

He stopped quite suddenly as his feet touched rock: the end of the tunnel. He turned over and sat up, more than half expectant of the Nazi guns somewhere in the total darkness, waiting for him. But when a voice came it was Xarchios's.

'All is well. There are no Nazis.'

Cameron said, 'Thank God for that. Have we far to go now, Xarchios?'

'Again the deadline! We shall make it – I have a boat, a fishing boat—'

'We have to get out of here first, haven't we? How do we climb that tunnel?'

'Patience and you will see.' Xarchios's face was close,

though totally invisible: the smell of garlic swept Cameron's nostrils, strong and sour. 'Now we go on. Keep very near – here, take a hold of my belt, and do not let go. Whatever you do, do not let go, for if you become lost you will wander through the earth for ever until you die of starvation.'

They moved through the total invisibility, taking it slow. Cameron had never known such darkness; it seemed to enter his very soul, to press his eyeballs inwards, to inhibit all movement. But he set his teeth and moved on, cannoning into rock walls on either side, bumping his head painfully on downward-hanging projections. Xarchios was apparently moving by feel alone, stopping now and then to mutter to himself in his own language, then moving carefully on again. He passed instructions and guidance back to Cameron as they turned into side passages; another drop, a short one this time, came up ahead, revealed to Xarchios by a count of footsteps from a turn in the tunnel. Even with the Greek's warning, Cameron felt every bone in his body jar as he went over the three-foot drop suddenly and landed with unflexed legs. On again, down and down … the air was stale, close. He was sweating now, getting hotter himself though the cave's temperature was even. The sweat poured into his lacerations, stinging and burning. He fought down rising panic; would they ever get out? If anything should happen to Xarchios his number would be up for certain. His life would end in an eternity of blind blundering around in the earth's stomach, sealed, entombed … an unnatural end for a seaman! He fixed his mind ahead: if Xarchios lived, they would make it – Nazis permitting, of course – and he would rejoin his ship. He thought about the *Wharfedale*, cruising in the open sea clear of Kithnos. She too would be in continuing danger and would remain so until she was once again out of the Aegean and back in Cunningham's Pond, bound again for the Grand Harbour in Malta … a different sort of danger and one that Cameron would much prefer to be facing. It would be quite a moment, when they steamed back past Malta's breakwater, past Fort St Angelo through the bright blue water of the world above …

125

'Stop,' Xarchios said suddenly, keeping his voice low.

Cameron stopped.

Xarchios spoke again, turning to breathe more garlic into Cameron's ear. 'Von Rudsdorf is in a side cave leading off the passage when we turn one more corner. That is, he should be.'

'Should be?'

'The Nazis may have moved him. I think this is possible, for there is no sound from ahead, and we are close enough to hear the movement of guards. If there are no guards, then there will be no von Rudsdorf. Also, I would expect light, and there is no light.'

'So what do we do?'

Xarchios said, 'I shall go on and see what is to be seen. You will stay here, and not move. I will take my gun now.'

'But I—'

'There will be no buts, no argument.' The tone was final. 'For now I am in charge and you will do as I say. I know the cave system like the back of my hand, which the Nazis do not and nor do you. Do not move a finger or a foot – or your tongue. I shall be back quickly.'

Cameron was aware of Xarchios moving away from him: the aloneness struck home forcibly. He sweated more than ever. The silence was as total as the darkness. Xarchios knew how to move without making a sound. It was almost as though Cameron was bereft of two of his senses. The wait seemed endless, and imagination expanded: Xarchios would walk into a trap and that would be the finish.

But Xarchios did not walk into a trap. As promised, he was quickly back: as he felt for Cameron's presence with outstretched fingers, Xarchios said, 'I have von Rudsdorf with me. He was never found by the Nazis, who have not been here long I believe. We have been lucky! The cave system is complicated, and our partisans had left the German bound. He is still gagged and his wrists still tied—'

'How do we get him out?' Cameron asked urgently. 'We can't climb back up the tunnel, surely?'

'No, no. That would be impossible. We fight him out,' Xarchios said. 'I have two things: my sub-machine-gun, and the advantage of complete surprise. The German will go in the middle – I have released his ankles – and you will hold tight to him, and follow.'

'To the main entrance, where we—?'

'Exactly so,' Xarchios interrupted. 'It will be a surprise attack from the rear, you see. Now we go.'

They moved off with the captive von Rudsdorf between them. It was a long trek through continuing darkness, but the Greek's sense of direction, his close knowledge of the cave system, was equal to it. The small procession turned many corners, climbed in places, descended again in others, pressing on for the exit. They moved fast; even Xarchios now seemed to have some regard for Cameron's rendezvous with the destroyer. At long last, they found glimmerings of light ahead at the end of a narrow tunnel along which they had to move bent almost double. The Greek whispered back over his shoulder to Cameron.

'The light of torches. The Nazis are there.'

'Are they near the exit?'

'Very close, yes. I think they watch for another approach, a frontal one. Soon there will be action. You are ready?'

'Ready,' Cameron said.

'Good! You will keep behind me, and watch the German carefully. He must not get away now.'

They moved fast still, but Xarchios slowed a little as they came towards the end of the tunnel, then he stopped. From behind him Cameron could see the backs of three German soldiers, armed and obviously on the alert as they faced the exit, which now stood out as the moonlight streamed through. As Cameron watched, another man joined the group, an NCO. Xarchios said, 'Four at least . . . perhaps many more. We shall see. Now it is speed that will count. That, and the surprise which will be very great. When I run, you run. We must be very careful to keep together, you understand?'

'Yes,' Cameron said, feeling the increased thump of his

heart. Behind the German, he moved on, not fast yet. Xarchios was waiting his moment. The Greek halted once more, just inside the tunnel's end, but only very briefly for a final reconnaissance. Then, with the Nazi's backs still turned towards him, he came out at the rush, firing his sub-machine-gun in a sweeping arc as he ran, Cameron gripping von Rudsdorf and forcing him on behind the Greek. All four soldiers fell, virtually colandered by the rapid fire. Xarchios and the other two were out of the cave, into the open air and the moonlight, almost before the last German had gone down in his pool of blood. They ran like the wind, but there was no pursuit. Evidently they had got the lot.

As he ran, Cameron glanced at his watch: a little after 0230 hours. One and a half hours to go.

'The fishing boat,' Xarchios said as they reached the coast. 'It has sails and it has an engine also. When we are well offshore, I shall start the engine. Not until then.'

'But we'll be seen in any case. Why not make all speed from the start?'

Xarchios grinned. 'The moon, yes. It is unkind, is that moon. But we met no one between the cave and here ... I have told you already, the Nazis' presence on Kithnos is small. We may be seen, but I believe we shall not be. If we are, then it is not unusual for fishing boats to leave before the dawn – but when there is wind, they do not use their engines. There *is* wind, as you can see ... and engine sounds might attract some attention. So no engines at the start.'

'All right,' Cameron said, shrugging. 'We'll do it your way, Xarchios. Where's the boat?'

'Close to where you landed. Come!'

Xarchios moved on. They came round a jut of rock and found a shallow bay. Xarchios's boat could be seen in the moonlight; it was small but adequate. They went forward and as they closed the boat Xarchios prodded von Rudsdorf with his sub-machine-gun. 'I shall cut away the rope on your wrists,' he said, 'and you will lend your weight to launch my boat. If you try to escape I shall shoot you in both your legs and you will be crippled. Do you understand?'

The German, still gagged, nodded: he spoke English, evidently. Xarchios brought out a knife and sliced through the rope around the wrists; von Rudsdorf rubbed life back into his hands. All three got around the boat and pushed it towards the water, which was covered with small wavelets brought up by the breeze as night slipped towards dawn. Scanning the horizon on the expected bearing, Cameron found no sign of the *Wharfedale*. When the fishing boat was waterborne, Xarchios saw von Rudsdorf over the gunwale, then got aboard himself with Cameron and ran up the sail, which soon filled with the wind; they stood offshore, setting course north-westward to Cameron's directions. He exulted in the feeling of being back at sea, free of the cave's terrible constriction and the feeling of claustrophobia which it gave. There was freedom in the wind itself, the wind that was carrying them nicely clear of Kithnos and its Nazi occupation. Xarchios was anxious to meet Razakis again, as he now said.

'Razakis is a good friend, a good fighter for Greece. To join him will be much pleasure to me. And with von Rudsdorf in his hands, Razakis will be able to change the course of history, and bring the power of the Soviets to the assistance of Greece, and drive out the Nazis!'

'I hope you're right,' Cameron said. 'It seems to me that Russia's going to be pretty fully occupied in dealing with Hitler's invasion ... whether or not Comrade Stalin gets the warning ahead.'

'When Hitler knows Comrade Stalin has got it,' Xarchios said, 'he may change his plans!'

Cameron doubted the proposition, but said no more. It was not up to him to dampen Xarchios's hopes; the guerrilla's homeland of Greece was everything to him, and Cameron wished him and his fellow-countrymen the best of luck in the casting-off of the Nazi yoke. In Britain, they still didn't know what it was to be occupied – yet. The day could come, but with the immensity of the Soviet Union on their side it would be unlikely. Cameron, fully realizing the importance of getting von Rudsdorf into Russian territory so that his vital information could be repeated in person, stared ahead across the as yet dark waters: still no *Wharfedale*, and now the dawn was not far off and the sea would soon lighten dangerously.

He was about to urge Xarchios to use his engines when the Greek, turning his head to look back towards the coast, gave a sudden exclamation. Cameron looked round: a boat was leaving the shore, a power boat coming up fast on their port quarter, throwing up a bow-wave and wake clearly visible as brilliant streaks of green phosphorescence. 'Now the engine!' Xarchios said, and busied himself in the stern of the boat. After some preliminary coughs, the outboard engine stuttered into life; it didn't, in fact, appear to make much difference to their speed – not enough, anyway, to compete with the boat coming up astern. A voice, a guttural voice speaking German, shouted through an amplified loud-hailer, and Xarchios, his face contorted with fury, made an obscene gesture towards the power boat. As he held his course and speed, the firing started. Bullets zipped across, but fell harmlessly into the sea astern. The fishing boat was not yet quite within range, but it was only a matter of minutes now. As the gap closed fast, the boat's sail showed a line of holes. The power boat, now very nearly abeam, had them well in its sights. Xarchios gave a roar of sudden pain and slumped across the gunwale with his head sagging into the sea; Cameron, needing all his strength to do so, dragged the Greek back into the well of the boat. The face was a mess: the jaw had been ripped off and blood was flowing freely. The Greek's curses were indistinct, and were cut off finally when another burst of fire, cutting through the boat's flimsy sides, smashed into his head and neck.

'Did you hear that, sir?' Drummond, on the compass platform of the *Wharfedale*, swung his glasses to the bearing.

'I did, Number One. Machine-gun fire, I fancy. Coming from around the cape ahead there.' Sawbridge looked at the gyro repeater for a moment, then passed his orders. 'Starboard ten ... steady! Full ahead both engines.'

He stepped away from the binnacle; he had approached Kithnos on a different course from his first run in, and had a jut of land between his ship and the point where he had landed Cameron, his idea being to keep concealed from the departure beach for as long as possible. Now his presence might well be needed, and it was time to show. Using his glasses as the destroyer, under full power and throwing up a massive bow-wave, began to move round the cape, he picked up the two boats.

He turned to Drummond. 'Searchlight, Number One,' he ordered tersely. 'Stand by all guns' crews.'

The orders were quickly passed; the searchlight flickered into life and was beamed on to the gun-battle ahead. The boats came up brilliantly lit, every detail clear. In the fishing boat Cameron could be seen, pumping away with Xarchios's sub-machine-gun. In the power boat were Nazi uniforms. So fierce was the battle that as yet no one appeared to be reacting to the searchlight. Sawbridge, gripping the forward guardrail tightly, passed the helm orders to ram and sink. Sweeping on, with his close-range weapons' crews ready at their triggers, he saw the German faces as at last the *Wharfedale* herself was seen behind the searchlight. They showed stark fear and utter astonishment in the second or two before the destroyer hit. The power boat was taken flat amidships and carried on, in disintegrating pieces, by the destroyer's thrusting stem. Those pieces fell away as flotsam from the bows and the German bodies were swept aft to be mangled in the fast-turning screws. Sawbridge waited a moment then stopped engines. He brought *Wharfedale* round to port, coming up astern of the fishing boat, and gave Cameron a wave.

'Well done!' he shouted down. 'Have you got that bloody Nazi, von Rudsdorf?'

'Yes, sir. And alive, too!'

'Right. You'd better abandon ship pronto and I'll lower a boat. The sooner we're out of here, the better I'll like it.'

131

Sawbridge swung round as the First Lieutenant called to him. 'What is it, Number One?' Then he saw what had attracted Drummond's attention: a long, low silhouette had appeared on the horizon to the north-west and was turning bows-on to make an approach. 'A bloody destroyer ... and a pound to a penny it won't be one of ours! Get the seaboat away at once, Number One, and for God's sake don't let's have any dilly-dallying! Warn the Torpedo-Gunner ... I may go in and use his tin fish.'

13

CAMERON and von Rudsdorf were brought aboard in double-quick time and the seaboat was hoisted to the davits and left swung out. The fishing boat drifted away, still carrying Xarchios's mangled body. The moment the seaboat was clear of the water, Sawbridge swung his ship towards the destroyer, now racing in to engage. Her silhouette had been identified by now; she was an enemy right enough, an Italian. Sawbridge had made his final decision not to attempt a running battle with his after guns out of action, but to go in and fire off his torpedoes. At the tubes, Mr Vibart, Gunner (T), spat on his hands with much relish and anticipation. His torpedoes were in first-class trim and would run true ... he almost knew them all by name, in a manner of speaking, very intimately and with much affection. He would be sorry to see them go, but it was their duty, their purpose in life, to go; and so far in this war Mr Vibart hadn't had much chance to fire off his tubes. It had become largely a war of bloody aircraft, unsusceptible to torpedoes, the buggers ... now he had his chance and he was going to show what he could do, what he had been trained to do since the day he'd first opted for the torpedo branch as a seaman torpedoman. He spat on his hands again and glanced at his Torpedo-Gunner's Mate.

'All right, eh, Charlie?'

'All right, sir.'

'Let's bloody wop it 'em!' Mr Vibart said. 'Bloody Eyeties! Get the buggers before they piss off!'

'I don't reckon they're going to piss off,' the TGM said sourly: he had seen the still-distant flash from the Italian's fo'c'sle, and seconds later both he and the Gunner (T) and all the tubes' crews were drenched with seawater as the shell registered a near miss. Then another.

'Strewth!' Mr Vibart said unbelievingly. 'Never known the Eyeties to shoot so bloody straight. What's the skipper up to, I wonder?'

He had his answer within the next ten seconds as *Wharfedale* opened with her forward 4.7s. The ship vibrated to the crash and recoil of the guns as the charges exploded, sending the projectiles winging across towards the enemy. No hits were registered; each target, bows-on, was small to its opponent. But as the Italian's rangetaking and laying improved, a shell took *Wharfedale* close along her port side and exploded just below the bridge by the Carley float stowage. The structural damage was superficial but the casualties along the upper deck were heavy. Bloodied strips of flesh hung from broken steelwork below the bridge, and farther aft two of Mr Vibart's torpedomen were badly lacerated by shell splinters. On the compass platform, Sawbridge decided it was time to throw off the Italian's gunners by some zig-zagging before coming in on a steady course to fire off his torpedoes. The zig-zag seemed to be effective; the firing became a shade wild. As the two destroyers closed, Sawbridge prepared to start his torpedo run.

'Stand by tubes,' he ordered. At the tubes Mr Vibart got the message via the communication number's head-set. He nodded at the TGM: the stand-by warning was passed to the crews. The show was about to start. As *Wharfedale* rushed on to pass the Italian starboard to starboard, the gun-battle intensified; the British destroyer seemed to run in under an umbrella of shells from the Italian's main armament. As the two bows approached, with the ships some eight cables apart, the Italian seemed at last to comprehend Sawbridge's intentions, and she began a swing to port just as Sawbridge passed the executive down to the tubes.

Mr Vibart's response was immediate. His voice rose over the sound of the continuing gunfire: *'Fire one ... fire two ... fire three!'*

As the tubes hissed and the torpedoes plopped into the water Mr Vibart stood and watched their runs. They were true; the dawn was coming up fast now, and for a while he could follow the trails through the sea. But of course the perishing Eyetie had turned away: Mr Vibart swore viciously. His lovely, lethal torpedoes, finned and fish-shaped and engined, were all going to be wasted. But were they? Something was happening to the Eyetie: there was an explosion of a shell aft and she swung farther to port.

Mr Vibart snatched off his steel helmet and waved it in the air. 'Our lads got the bugger's screws with the 4.7s, Charlie! She's not under control!'

The TGM nodded: it had been a slice of luck. The Italian was coming round slap into the paths of the running fish, and she was set fair to get her guts blown out. The torpedomen watched, Vibart using his binoculars to try to keep a view of the tracks, but he had lost them now. However, a moment later twin explosions, one for'ard, one aft, came from the Italian. Bright red flame burgeoned, there was a devilish roar, and thick smoke rose. For a moment the destroyer seemed almost to rise in the air, then to take a list to port, with men dropping from her decks into the sea. In the next moment she had settled with her main deck awash, and then she had gone.

Mr Vibart looked across at the scene soberly. Two out of three – that wasn't bad in any Gunner (T)'s book! But now the thing was over, there was little rejoicing even if there was satisfaction in training having paid off. No seaman really liked to see the end of a ship, nor to witness human agony. Vibart listened to the weird silence that had replaced the crash of gunfire. The communication number, attending to his headphones, said, 'From the Captain, sir. Well done and congratulations.'

Vibart nodded, and passed the message where he felt it belonged: to the TGM and his torpedomen. Then he said,

'I reckon we'll be picking up survivors. Best get the scrambling-nets over the side.'

The TGM lifted a hand and pointed. Vibart saw two more enemy destroyers, distant but moving in. There would be no picking up of survivors, but there would be more action and he had to get his tubes ready again. As he passed the orders, *Wharfedale* swung hard to starboard and her engines, which had slowed after the Italian had gone down, came up again to full power as she steadied on a due easterly course.

On the bridge Sawbridge had reached a decision that might have serious political consequences but which he believed to be the only option now open to him. Von Rudsdorf and the Greek, Razakis, had to come before a possibly avoidable engagement with superior forces. Such avoidance, if Sawbridge could keep *Wharfedale* ahead of the destroyers' gun-range for long enough, could come via Turkish waters and two birds could be killed with one stone. Currently, he was something like 150 miles from the nearest point in Turkish territorial waters, and this he could reach in four hours – always assuming the enemy destroyers didn't overtake, of course, and he believed they hadn't the speed to do that.

It could be done.

'Tricky, sir,' Drummond said.

'I know. The Turks are teetering ... right now, they're still neutral, and it's a violation.'

'And a tight-rope,' Drummond said. He expanded: 'You seem to be banking on a belief that the Eyeties will respect Turkey's neutrality even though we'll have broken it wide open. You believe they'll leave us alone ... they just may not, sir. In which case—'

'In which case nothing's gained – I know! But I do believe they won't follow us in, at any rate not without orders from above. And I don't believe they're at all likely to be ordered in. The official Axis view will be that since the British have broken neutrality, the Turks'll move into Hitler's camp.'

Drummond said drily, 'Which they may!'

'I know the risks, Number One. But if Churchill's behind Razakis, as he's said to be ... well, what better backing could I have if things go wrong?'

Drummond said no more; the Captain's mind was made up, however dangerously, however foolishly. The Turks themselves might be well entitled to open fire on any invader of their neutrality; no doubt the Captain would have considered that. And no doubt his answer would be that he was prepared to take that risk too. It was not up to a First Lieutenant to argue further. *Wharfedale* rushed on, keeping – so far – out of range of the pursuit. Action stations were maintained; and Sawbridge used the tannoy to broadcast his decision to his ship's company. He was heading, he told them, for Turkish waters off Kusadasi behind the Aegean island of Vathi. That was all. Further decisions would be made known in due course.

After that he sent for Razakis and Cameron. Razakis was wary, withdrawn: he assumed, correctly, that Sawbridge had now made up his mind finally to land him in Turkey, and he was far from happy.

'The Turks are enemies,' he insisted once again, fiercely. 'I cannot trust them!'

'You won't have to,' Sawbridge said, smiling. 'That is, you *may* not have to. Not on your own, anyway. But I assume it still remains vital to get both you and von Rudsdorf into Russian hands?'

Razakis stared. 'Of course – most certainly! Why do you need to ask that, Captain?'

Sawbridge didn't answer the question directly, parrying it with one of his own. 'Worth the risk ... worth *any* risk, Razakis? I must know positively.'

Razakis narrowed his eyes, and pulled at his heavy beard. 'What risk do you refer to, Captain?'

'A risk perhaps equally as great as *not* taking von Rudsdorf through to Russia. I must make an assessment, you see. I'm sure you'll understand that, Razakis. Risk is your trade too, isn't it?'

Razakis gave a heavy nod. 'Yes.'

'Right, then I'll put it to you.' Sawbridge spoke briskly now; after much harrowing thought and the weighing of risks, he had returned to an earlier hypothesis and now saw it as the best way, indeed the only way of completing his mission. Currently under pursuit by the Italians, with the Germans well and truly alerted now as to his purpose, it would be quite impossible for him to run back and attempt to land his passengers on the Greek mainland or any of the Greek islands which, if he did land them, they might never be able to leave alive. There was just the one alternative, and he put it to Razakis bluntly.

He said, 'I propose to run north, right up the Turkish coast, keeping as close inside Turkish territorial waters as I can. At Cape Helles I shall enter the Dardanelles for the Sea of Marmara—'

Razakis swore. 'This you cannot do—'

'I can try, Razakis! Just hear me out. I shall cross the Sea of Marmara and enter the Bosporus, then the Black Sea. In the Black Sea, I shall make contact with Russian ships – there'll be no difficulty about that providing I can persuade them not to open fire – and hand you and von Rudsdorf over to Russian custody for immediate transfer to the Kremlin.' Sawbridge paused and wiped sweat from his face. 'How's that?'

Razakis gave a loud laugh. 'Crazy!' he said. 'Always the British suggest things that are crazy! How do you think you can enter either the Dardanelles or the Bosporus, Captain? Your ship – and von Rudsdorf, and I – all will be blown to small pieces by the Turkish guns!'

'It doesn't necessarily follow,' Sawbridge said mildly. 'But, since you do understand the risk involved, I just want to ask you this: is von Rudsdorf really worth that risk? I ask because it seems to me that if Stalin hasn't already seen through Hitler's little games, he hasn't much time left now to do anything about them in any case?'

'No, no, no!' Razakis shook his head with much emphasis.

138

'If nothing else, Captain, von Rudsdorf will be invaluable to Comrade Stalin for the knowledge that is in his head of the German dispositions and campaign plans and strengths of the formations that are to march against the Soviets. The answer to your question is yes. Any risk must be considered acceptable.'

'That's all I wanted to know,' Sawbridge said. He turned to Cameron. 'Sub, get hold of the Admiralty Sailing Directions for the Dardanelles. I'll want a complete picture of the approaches and defences – all right?'

Wharfedale kept ahead of the pursuing destroyers and in fact had drawn farther away from them by the time she made her entry into Turkish waters and was steaming behind the lee of Vathi. Once inside, Sawbridge altered course, as planned, to the north. The Italian destroyers came up, turning north in company when they were off *Wharfedale*'s port beam. Officers crowded their bridges, staring through binoculars at the British vessel. There seemed to be much consternation around, but so far at any rate no attempt was being made to follow in and violate Turkish sovereignty. Sawbridge had a feeling that this was one up to him; solemnly, he took off his steel helmet and swept it across his chest in a bow. From the Italian leader's bridge, a fist was waved.

Sawbridge grinned. 'Flummoxed, I'd say! I think we can forget them for the time being, Number One.'

'Perhaps, sir, but not the Turks.'

'Who are currently conspicuous by their absence. We'll cross that bridge when we come to it, which I've no doubt we shall!' Sawbridge rubbed at tired eyes. 'Better arrange a relieve-decks for breakfast, Number One. The captains of the guns can send men below in relays, but all hands are to stand by for instant recall to stations.'

'Aye, aye, sir.' Drummond turned away to pass the orders to the Chief Boatswain's Mate and the Gunner's Mate, feeling in his bones, still, that the Captain was playing an extremely dangerous game. Violation of neutrality could have all manner of repercussions in the diplomatic field, and the diplomats were always pretty adept at pinning the blame on the armed services whenever they could. This time, they wouldn't need to try very hard. As Drummond went down the ladder from the bridge he saw that matters were about to come to a head: away to starboard, out from the coast near Kusadasi, a vessel was coming. It looked like a small gunboat; and already the starboard bridge lookout had reported to the Captain.

Drummond turned back up the ladder. Now the gunboat was signalling by lamp. The Yeoman of Signals was trying to read it, apparently without success. He reported to the Captain, 'Gibberish, sir.'

'Otherwise and more politely known as Turkish!' Sawbridge waved a hand towards the Italian destroyers on the port beam; they were prudently sheering off, putting more obvious distance between themselves and the Turkish limits. 'The Turks seem to have put the fear of Islam or whatever into the infidels, anyway!'

'And us, sir?' Drummond asked. 'The gunboat's probably ordering us to heave-to.'

'Very likely,' Sawbridge said. 'And heave-to we will – there's no point in being rude, I suppose!' He bent to the voice-pipe. 'Both engines to stop.'

Bells rang below. 'Engines repeated stopped, sir,' the Torpedo-Coxswain reported.

'Half astern both engines,' Sawbridge said. He straightened; as the way came off the ship he stopped engines again and waited. The gunboat, now seen positively to be such, steamed busily and amid clouds of black smoke towards the British destroyer, and when it was within hailing distance a small, fat man in a curious and colourful uniform began bawling through a megaphone. Like the lamp signal, it was gibberish, but the purport was clear enough: the British were being warned to go away or else. The fat man made shoo-ing motions with his hands and with the megaphone, then stepped down from his tiny bridge and ostentatiously patted the barrel of a small gun on his fo'c'sle. Then he turned the gun towards the *Wharfedale* and strutted back to the bridge.

Sawbridge said, 'We'll show willing.' He turned to the navigator. 'Pilot, do your level best to put me right slap bang on the territorial limit and keep me there – in fact, just a shade outside it if anything. All right? That should satisfy the Turk and I doubt if the Italians will take the risk of opening fire. While you're working it out, I'll move westerly.'

The orders were passed to take the destroyer on an obviously westerly course for a while, and she proceeded outwards at half speed. The gunboat made an attempt to follow, to shepherd the intruder away, but was soon left behind. When Bradley, the navigator, had worked out his intricate position, *Wharfedale*'s helm was put to starboard and her engines increased to full, and once again she proceeded on a northerly course. By Bradley's reckoning, they would be off Cape Helles and the Dardanelles entry within six hours. Sawbridge looked at his watch: 0635. By the time they made Cape Helles, there would be a reception committee waiting. Half an hour later, the w/t office reported the interception of coded wireless signals being transmitted by the Italian leader to an unknown destination: no doubt the British movements were being reported to whatever other enemy ships or aircraft were likely to be interested ... in the meantime, Cameron's study, along with the navigator, of the Sailing Directions, had revealed a strong defence of the approaches. This defence was almost certainly stronger than the Sailing Directions indicated: they were somewhat out of date since the declaration of war in 1939. Sawbridge found little hope of being able to crash through, though he was prepared to face that if he had to. He was possessed now of an iron determination to deliver Razakis and von Rudsdorf to the Russians. But in the first instance, some kind of diplomatic approach had to be attempted, and this also produced difficulties: Razakis was adamant that he was not going to have any dealings with the Turkish authorities; he said again that they were not to be trusted.

'They will hoodwink you, Captain. They will say they will

141

let your ship through the Dardanelles, and when you are inside, you will be arrested – and so will I, and von Rudsdorf. Again I say, it is crazy!'

'They can arrest us just as easily outside the Dardanelles, off Cape Helles—'

Razakis raised his fists in the air. 'Then do not approach Cape Helles! Go out to sea, and put me ashore in Greece!'

'That's not on,' Sawbridge said. He waved a hand to his port beam, where the Italian destroyers were still keeping him company. 'It's likely enough that the Stukas will be ordered up this way soon, to locate us. I've a feeling that our only chance lies here, and in the Dardanelles passage—'

'Then you feel as a fool!' Razakis shouted.

Sawbridge shrugged. 'Time will tell, Razakis. At least you're away from Greece and the Nazis. Be thankful for that, for God's sake!'

Once again, the tannoy gave the ship's company the facts: they were bound for the Dardanelles. The very word 'Dardanelles' held foreboding. In the last war, too many lives – British, Australian, New Zealand – had been thrown away upon those grim and bloody beaches. Winston Churchill had been behind that brave attempt, too, as First Lord of the Admiralty. Regiment after regiment, ship after ship, had been destroyed over the weary, battered months of 1916. One or two of the older hands had personal memories of the slaughter off Gallipoli, of ships sunk under them, of messmates screaming out their dying agonies in the holocaust of shot and shell, of the old steamer *River Clyde* and the troops she had sent ashore to wither under the machine-guns even before they had waded through the water to land. The Torpedo-Coxswain was one of these; he had been a seaman boy in the *Queen Elizabeth* then, and now, a chief petty officer at his action station on the wheel, he sucked his teeth gloomily at his memories. Another was Mr Vibart, then also a seaman boy first-class serving in a cruiser that had been sunk by the shore batteries. Now, wishing to talk to a fellow sufferer as it were, one who knew what it had been like, he climbed to the conning-tower for a natter, using his relieve-decks break to do so.

'Fair sod, 'Swain,' he said. 'You'll remember!'

'That I do,' the Torpedo-Coxswain agreed. 'Mind, it's different this time.'

'Yes. We're that much bloody older.' Vibart brought out a handkerchief and blew his nose. 'Got families to worry about, among other things.'

'So we had then, come to that. My mum worried herself sick.'

'You know what I mean, 'Swain.'

'Yes, I do, course I do, sir. But I don't reckon this is going to come to shooting. Skipper, he wouldn't take the ship into certain destruction.'

'What, then?' Vibart asked sarcastically.

The Torpedo-Coxswain said, 'Skipper'll find a way. He knows what to expect ... he wouldn't be heading for Cape Helles if he didn't think it was worth while, stands to reason.' He paused. 'Got something up his sleeve, I reckon ...'

'Well, I hope you're bloody right, 'Swain. We don't want last time all over again,' Vibart said, and went back down to his torpedo-tubes. He doubted if they would be needed off Cape Helles, or anyway he hoped they wouldn't, but they had to be on the top line just the same. That was his job, and his pride also – if it hadn't been, he would never have got his warrant. From his tubes, Mr Vibart looked out at the Italian destroyers, still steaming fast in company, waiting to see what happened, Vibart supposed. Breath hissed through his teeth: he would have liked nothing so much as to send his tin fish into each of the bastards! That Mussolini, 'Il Duce' as he called himself, was accustomed to refer to the Mediterranean as Mare Nostrum, Our Sea. He needed teaching a lesson; it was sheer bloody cheek. Why, the Med had been British ever since Nelson's time! Mr Vibart looked away from temptation and studied the Turkish coastline to starboard. It looked pretty rough, and in his time he'd heard some nasty stories about the Turks and their cruelties towards their enemies, and about their moral standards too, which were different from the British. And the things the Turkish women got up to as well on the field of battle when it was all over – like the Pathans along the North-West Frontier of India! The knives came out to be used on the dead and wounded, and nothing was sacred, nothing at all.

That would never do.

Better, much better, to go down fighting in the clean blue sea than to be, say, taken ashore for internment. And in Mr Vibart's view it was precisely internment that the skipper was heading for if he didn't watch out.

It was noon now, with some half an hour to go for Cape Helles, already in view ahead. North-eastward from the cape and its old fortified castle, Tree Peak rose 750 feet above the sea, while opposite Helles loomed the fortress of Cape Yen Shehr. The entry to the Dardanelles was heavily enough protected, and ships attempting the move inwards without authority would enter the very gates of hell. As he took his ship closer now into Turkish territorial waters Sawbridge, who was far from having anything up his sleeve as prognosticated by the Torpedo-Coxswain, was keeping an open mind: something that he acknowledged to himself to be a euphemism for not knowing what the devil to do next.

'At the start,' he said to Drummond, 'I'll let events dictate – see what happens, and then decide the next move.' He gave a sudden grin, a somewhat tight-lipped one. 'Masterly inactivity ... it often pays off!'

'Yes, sir. So does boldness. What we're doing is pretty bold, though the Admiralty may find another name for it later on.' Drummond paused, looking out ahead through his binoculars. 'What I mean is, the Turks are going to be God Almighty surprised—'

'Caught with their pants down?'

'Something like that, sir. If we go on being bold, we just may be able to talk our way through rather than start the shooting. There's nothing so effective as bullshit – sometimes!'

Sawbridge murmured, 'I was beginning to think the same way myself, as a matter of fact. Where's Cameron?' He turned. 'Ah – there you are, Sub. I may have a job for you.'

'Yes, sir?'

'I'll be more precise when I've provoked a reaction from the Turks. In the meantime, see that Razakis and von Rudsdorf are stowed away somewhere where they won't be found easily. And put a guard on them.'

'Aye, aye, sir.'

Cameron turned away and went down the ladder. As he left the compass platform things began happening from the shore. From Cape Helles a light began flashing and out from the entry to the narrows came three warships, two of them small gunboats, one of them an antique-looking destroyer. They moved out towards the *Wharfedale*. Sawbridge studied them through his binoculars, then turned his attention to the Italian destroyers' bridges. The officers were looking jubilant.

Sawbridge said, 'They're expecting us to be ordered out. That'll give them their chance.' He lowered his glasses and turned to Drummond. 'Fall out action stations, Number One.'

'Fall out, sir?' Drummond stared.

'That's what I said. We come in peace to a neutral country! Pipe, hands fall in for entering harbour ... and since I intend to anchor, you can pipe the cable party and special sea dutymen.'

14

To the ship's company it was a curious business: there was the enemy, all guns manned, just a half-mile or so to port, keeping unctuously clear of Turkish territorial waters; there were the Turks steaming towards them, also with guns manned; and they themselves were falling in fore and aft, hastily cleaned into the rig of the day, more or less, caps on square, hands clasped behind their backs in the at-ease position, their Divisional Officers standing in front of the ranks after a formal inspection to ensure that the men were as tidy as was possible in the circumstances. Proper peacetime – or anyway like entering Malta under the critical eyes of the Flag. Talk about bull!

There was plenty of *sotto voce* comment.

'Skipper's gorn round the bend, like Harpic.'

'Thinks 'e's comin' into bloody Pompey!'

'Eyeties'll be laughin' themselves sick.'

'Stop that yattering – keep silent!' This was the Gunner's Mate, who had suddenly gone all gas and gaiters, like on the parade ground at Whale Island, the gunnery heaven beloved of Gunner's Mates. 'Keep fell in proper an' eyes front, you've not bin told to stand *easy*. The order was stand *at ease*.' The seamen muttered, but understood the vital difference well enough. Sod the Turks ...

Wharfedale moved on, slap into the jaws of the unknown. On the bridge Sub-Lieutenant Bradley watched for his anchor bearings; in the eyes of the ship the Cable Officer stood with his red anchor flag ready, awaiting the Captain's order, the

146

port anchor already veered to the waterline and held on the brake.

As the bearings began to come on, the Captain raised his own red flag; the Cable Officer followed suit. When the navigator reported the ship in position, Sawbridge called sharply, '*Let go!*' and in the same instant brought his flag down, as did the Cable Officer. At the cable-holder the shipwright spun the brake off, and, with the Blake slip already knocked away, the cable rattled out in a cloud of red rust. Sawbridge brought her up at the third shackle, putting his engines briefly astern until her way was off. When the ship had got her cable he ordered the cable party and special sea dutymen to be fallen out. Then he turned to the Yeoman of Signals. He said, 'Make to Cape Helles: I request the hospitality of your waters for the statutory period as allowed under International Law.'

'Aye, aye, sir.' The message was sent out by light. After this there was a lengthy delay, during which the crews of the Turkish warships stared curiously from behind their guns. Sawbridge remarked that there might be a language difficulty in addition to the undoubted fact that contact would have to be made with Ankara; and the Turkish radio links could well be primitive. When the answer came back in English, it was simple and to the point: 'You must go to sea or be interned.'

'Helpful bastards!' Sawbridge said angrily. 'I thought at least they'd respect our own belligerent rights to ask for temporary shelter.'

'Could be because of the Italians, sir,' Drummond said.

'I don't see why,' Sawbridge snapped. 'Yeoman!'

'Sir?'

'Make: I intend landing an officer to discuss vital matters with the Military Governor in Gallipoli and expect you to accord me my proper rights. Any hostile act committed against me in the meantime will be considered most serious by the British Government and in particular by Winston

Churchill. That's all.' Sawbridge turned to Cameron. 'You'll be the officer, Sub.'

Possibly it was the use of Churchill's name, possibly it was the fact that the Turkish Government was more than half inclined towards Britain and wished to establish good relations; whatever it was, a signal came back after another long delay to say that a British officer would be permitted to land and would be transported by road along the forty-seven miles from Cape Helles to Gallipoli at the inward end of the Dardanelles passage. In the meantime the British destroyer was to remain at her anchorage with her guns unmanned and trained peacefully to the fore-and-aft line. Any deviation from this would result in her being ordered to sea forthwith. A power boat would be sent to bring off the officer to Cape Helles, and he would be returned when the meeting with the Military Governor ended.

'Watch your step,' Sawbridge advised Cameron, 'and your tongue. You'll be on your own – I won't know what's happening to you, and you'll have to be careful not to provoke the Turks. That apart, you have *carte blanche*. Your job's simple in basis – you've got to get approval for me to move through to the Black Sea. That's all. And the best of luck!'

Cameron saluted and went down to the quarterdeck to await the boat from Cape Helles. It arrived hard on the heels of the signal, and Cameron seated himself in the sternsheets under the close scrutiny of its crew – four Turkish seamen, all armed to the teeth and looking as brigandish as Razakis and the other Greek partisans. The boat had just cast off from the destroyer's side when the Captain on the bridge received a report that six aircraft had been sighted, coming in from the south. Bringing up his glasses, he identified them quickly.

'Stukas,' he said. 'I'll give them the benefit of the doubt – nothing precipitate, or Cameron may suffer.'

From the decks, all hands watched the incoming German dive-bombers; every man holding his breath, wondering what the pilots' intentions might be. In they came, quite clearly now making for the anchorage. Sawbridge said, 'The Italians will have brought them in – those wireless signals we intercepted. I don't like it, Number One.'

'Diving!' Drummond shouted suddenly. Sawbridge's hand, already hovering over the action alarm, pressed it. The rattlers sounded throughout the destroyer, and her decks came alive as the men doubled to their action stations and began to swing the anti-aircraft armament up to meet the diving Stukas. Seconds later, the first bombs screamed down. Two hit the Turkish destroyer, putting her ablaze fore and aft. Men began jumping into the sea from her decks. Waterspouts surrounded *Wharfedale* as Sawbridge passed urgent orders to weigh and get on the move. Then a bomb took the destroyer slap on the torpedo-tubes. There was an almighty explosion. When the smoke and debris cleared a little, the remains of bodies were to be seen everywhere; Vibart lay with arms and legs gone, a twitching, agonized trunk that had little time to live, mouth open and screaming on a high note. Sawbridge, his face white as a sheet, picked up a megaphone and shouted across the water to Cameron.

'Rejoin!' he called. 'Those buggers ... I'm taking advantage of the situation they've created and balls to British violation ... I'm going into the Dardanelles!'

Wharfedale swept under full power for the narrows; Cameron had dived in from the Turkish boat and swum for the ship's side, to be grappled aboard aft. The Turkish boat's crew were too panic-stricken even to notice he'd gone. The Italian destroyers were lying off still; they had not opened in support of their German allies, leaving it, perhaps, to the Nazis to incur the opprobrium of the Turks. The Stukas followed the British ship for a little way, then suddenly broke off as Sawbridge had gambled they would, and climbed and spiralled away over the Aegean; to drop their bomb-loads closer to the Dardanelles entry would be foolish, and would negate the claim that they would no doubt make – that they had not known the British ship was inside Turkish territorial waters.

As the Stukas made off, Sawbridge ordered his anti-aircraft weapons to cease fire and called for damage reports. In addition to the loss of the torpedo-tubes, there was a great, gaping hole in the upper deck, a hole that descended to the officers' cabins, all of which had been totally destroyed by the explosion and the resulting fire, which now had the hoses on it and was dimming down. The wardroom itself had gone as well, as had the pantry. There was a good deal of ancillary damage on deck but this was mostly superficial and the ship was seaworthy and under full command.

The anchorage was in total confusion as *Wharfedale* sped through. Boats of all shapes and sizes were coming out from Cape Helles and other places, a veritable regatta, with collisions everywhere as the Turks charged into each other's courses. Baggy-trousered men were shouting and gesticulating, firing off revolvers to no apparent purpose; and now the Italian warships were turning to depart. Events, perhaps, had moved somewhat beyond them and discretion was now the better part of valour: no doubt in their eyes the British destroyer was in any case moving into an impossible position.

Sawbridge stood behind the binnacle, conning his ship into the narrow passage of the Dardanelles. The forts stood silent as the *Wharfedale* went by with her remaining guns manned and ready. In the constricted waters, she could not move at speed; as Sawbridge brought the engines down, a consuming impatience laid hold of him. More fortresses lay ahead, mostly ancient monuments but ones that could have been modernized and re-armed: New Castle of Asia at Koum Kaleh was the next past Cape Yen Shehr, and then others before they reached Gallipoli. Anything might happen; even if no fire was opened earlier, the destroyer could be stopped in her tracks by gunfire from Gallipoli before she reached the Sea of Marmara. But in the meantime there was no interference with her passage; as they went past more modern defences the guns stayed silent, and here and there a hand waved in apparently friendly fashion. Certainly, after the bombing and sinking in the anchorage outside, there would be little Turkish love left for the Nazis ...

'Depending on what happens in Gallipoli, Sub,' Sawbridge said as he watched the waters ahead, 'I may decide to put you ashore with Razakis and von Rudsdorf.'

Cameron asked, 'You're not going to try for entry to the Black Sea, then, sir?'

'I don't know yet. A lot must depend ... as I said.'

'Yes, sir.' Cameron cleared his throat somewhat hesitantly. Then he said, 'Razakis won't land in Gallipoli, sir.'

'Razakis may have to change his bloody tune, Sub!'

'He's adamant, sir. I'm quite convinced he won't shift.'

Sawbridge laughed; it was an edgy sound. 'He'll be bloody well landed with an armed escort if that's what I decide to do,' he said. 'I've already stuck my neck out so far I'll never get it back in again!'

'Yes, sir.' Cameron coughed discreetly. 'I believe that if we put Razakis ashore against his will, he'll simply refuse to co-operate—'

'Balls,' Sawbridge said briefly. 'Whatever he is, he's a Greek and a patriot. He'll put his country's interest first – and his communism!'

'Not in Turkey, sir. He'll never talk to the Turks ... and there's no Russians available to him.' Cameron paused, then went on with emphasis. 'I'm absolutely certain I'm right, sir.'

'As every officer should be,' Sawbridge said with a grin. 'There's nothing like self-confidence!'

Cameron flushed. 'I'm sorry, sir. I didn't mean to sound—'

'Cocky? As a matter of fact, you didn't, Sub. But you did sound convinced, I'll say that. Further, I agree Razakis is an obstinate bastard to put it mildly. I may find another way, but—' Sawbridge broke off as a report reached him from one of the lookouts.

'Gallipoli in sight, sir!'

Sawbridge nodded. 'Thank you.' He looked ahead through his binoculars, then stepped to the tannoy and made the switch. 'This is the Captain speaking,' he said into the microphone. 'We are now approaching Gallipoli, a name that I know some of you have memories of. Forget them. I don't propose to storm the beaches. I doubt if we shall be attacked, but they may try to arrest us. If they do, I shall rely on talk to get us out. I have to remember Turkey's status as a neutral power. That's all for now.'

He flicked off the switch. Ahead, the Gallipoli defences loomed, giving the lie to the peace inherent in the domes and minarets and towers of the city, lying pink and gold and purple above the blue water, an aspect of history and of pure romance. It was a brilliant day, not a cloud to break the sky, and the colouring was magnificent. But one wrong move now, and the colours might dissolve into the raw red of running blood and the orange flashes of the guns amid the smoke. . . .

'Boat approaching, sir,' Cameron said.

Sawbridge nodded. Lifting his binoculars again, he studied the boat, coming fast towards the destroyer under power. There was an important-looking officer seated beneath a canopy, with a civilian in a white suit. 'All right, Number One,' Sawbridge said. 'Bring 'em aboard if that's what they want.'

Drummond clattered down the ladder after sending the bridge messenger for the Chief Boatswain's Mate, and made his way aft to receive the Turks. No word had come from the Captain as to falling out from action stations; the guns' crews remained closed-up as the *Wharfedale* moved on, her engines now at slow ahead. A moment after Drummond had left the bridge, Sawbridge gave the order for the engines to be stopped, and the destroyer drifted on to lie off the port and await the embarkation of the Turkish VIPs. Sawbridge said, 'Now or never, Sub.'

'Yes, sir. Are you going to send Razakis and von Rudsdorf ashore with the Turks, sir?'

'I don't know yet. I'll see how things develop.'

They waited; as the way came off the destroyer, the boat from Gallipoli came alongside. Sawbridge moved to the starboard guardrail of the bridge and stood for a moment at the salute. He called down, 'You are welcome to board my ship, gentlemen.'

The two men had come out from the canopy and were standing now in the sternsheets. The uniformed officer called up in excellent English, 'We shall not board, Captain. The guns of the fortress are trained upon your ship and if you do not anchor you will be in danger of being sunk. You are in violation of our neutrality.'

'So were the Germans, off Cape Helles.'

'Yes. With this I agree—'

'And your government is known to be moving closer towards an understanding with Britain. I'm no diplomat, I admit . . . but it seems to me that your anger should be turned against Hitler rather than us.' Sawbridge paused, his decision hardening fast. 'I come in peace, asking only to be allowed to proceed through your waters into the Black Sea.'

There was a hasty consultation between the uniformed man and the civilian, then the officer called back, 'Russia is your enemy! I do not understand. In the Black Sea you will be apprehended by Soviet warships.'

Sawbridge said, 'Not if I remain in your territorial waters outside the Bosporus. I'm hopeful your neutrality won't be invaded by three powers! I have an important message that must be passed without delay to the Kremlin. It must be passed in person.'

'It cannot be permitted,' the officer said.

'If you do not permit it, you will give vital aid to the Nazis. That is not in the spirit of neutrality under International Law.'

'It cannot be permitted,' the Turk said again. There was a ring of finality, of no further argument. 'I am instructed by my government in Ankara that your ship is to be arrested and brought into the port of Gallipoli, and that you and your seamen are to be disembarked and held in internment until the war is ended.' He paused. 'If you should resist arrest, then I am empowered to take whatever measures appear necessary. This could mean that the shore batteries will open on you. I wish your answer immediately.'

Sawbridge stared down at the Turks. The situation was a diabolical one. To submit to internment was unthinkable. His mission, after all the difficulties and dangers that were behind them, would remain totally unfulfilled, with world-shaking results. Yet the alternative was serious enough as well. Sawbridge swallowed and called down to the boat. 'Who is to give the order to open fire on me, if I refuse?'

'I am. I am ready to give it. I am ready now.'

Sawbridge said, 'If you do, you will regret it. I am under orders from my government, not to break your neutrality certainly, but to deliver my message to the Russians. Your government will confirm that Winston Churchill in particular wishes good relations with Turkey, and your country stands in imminent danger of a massive German attack. If that should happen, then Turkey will be glad enough to have my country on her side. To sink a British destroyer would be unfortunate.'

'Then,' the Turk called back, 'your answer is no, Captain?'

'Dead correct!' Sawbridge said savagely. The Turks were bluffing – they had to be; but it was quite clear that Gallipoli would after all be no place to land Razakis with his vital information. The Greek would be blocked for far too long. Sawbridge swung away, his mouth hard. Down the voice-pipe he said, 'Engines to full ahead.' Then he flicked the tannoy on. 'I'm taking her through,' he said to his ship's company. 'All the way to the Black Sea.'

Boldness paid, so far at any rate: the guns on Gallipoli stayed silent as the *Wharfedale* passed through the port at speed and entered the land-locked Sea of Marmara with her remaining armament still closed-up and ready, though Sawbridge had passed the word that any trigger-happiness would result in cell punishment when they returned to join the Fleet in Malta. He was determined not to fire upon the Turks or their installations whatever might be thrown at him from the defences. At least he would keep his nose clean to that extent. There was

154

no interference in the Sea of Marmara either, though behind them a Turkish destroyer emerged from Gallipoli and thereafter kept in company astern. *Wharfedale* made the 140-mile passage to the Bosporus in good time, arriving off Istanbul within four hours of passing Gallipoli. Whilst in the Sea of Marmara Sawbridge had sent, via his wireless transmitter, a plain-language signal addressed as a general message to any Russian warships in the southern sector of the Black Sea, asking for a rendezvous off the mouth of the Bosporus. At Istanbul, there was watchfulness from the shore but they were allowed to enter the narrow waterway without hindrance, the Turkish destroyer entering behind them.

By late afternoon Sawbridge had the northern end of the Bosporus in sight. Cameron was on the bridge when Bradley spotted the funnels and fighting-tops of a Russian cruiser lying ahead, distantly, obviously keeping well clear of Turkish waters. As they emerged into the Black Sea the Russian's signal lamps started calling, asking for identification.

'Spell out our name, Yeoman,' Sawbridge said. 'Add, I am sending a boat to the territorial limit. Request you do likewise.' He turned to Cameron. 'Right, Sub. I'll approach the limit within a quarter of a mile – no closer. As we come up, I'll call away the seaboat. Have Razakis and von Rudsdorf standing by.'

Wharfedale moved on at slow speed and ten minutes later her engines were put astern to bring her up. As she drifted, the seaboat was slipped with Razakis and von Rudsdorf embarked and pulled ahead towards the Russian boat, which had come off from the cruiser's side as the British boat took the water. The Russian had moved closer in now, and from *Wharfedale*'s bridge her ship's company could be seen lining her rails and staring in wonder at what was going on. Cameron's boat pulled strongly for the rendezvous on the three-mile territorial limit. Razakis was looking happy at last, though he kept casting glances astern at the hovering Turkish destroyer as though at any moment she might rush towards him and frustrate his purpose.

The boats approached within hailing distance, and from the Russian an officer called in hesitant English, 'You come closer to us, yes?'

'All right,' Cameron called back, not too happily. No actual lines could be drawn upon the sea; it was a matter of mutual trust now – they could be inside Turkish waters or upon the Russian-dominated open sea, and their two countries were as yet at war. 'You come towards us as well, yes?'

'Yes.'

They moved closer; Razakis, preparing for the final transfer, held out a hand. Cameron took it; the Greek's clasp was warm and there was gratitude in his eyes and in his voice as he said his goodbyes.

'You are a brave man and a good one. I thank you with all my heart for what you have done for Greece.'

'It'll help my country as well, Razakis – what *you* have done. Perhaps the world, who knows?'

Razakis smiled and nodded and once again gripped Cameron's hand. Then the boats came together, lifting and falling against the fenders. Razakis stepped across, assisted now by Russian hands. Von Rudsdorf followed, politely treated by the Russian seamen: he was still their ally. As soon as the two men were aboard, the Russian boat pulled back to the cruiser. Waves were exchanged, and for a few moments Cameron watched the boat moving fast across the Black Sea with its vital secrets in the heads of the Greek and the German. Then he nodded to his Coxswain to head back for the *Wharfedale*.

The Turkish port authorities made no more trouble all the way back through the Bosporus and the Dardanelles. Passing Gallipoli again that night, there was total silence from the shore, almost as though they were being ignored, a blind eye turned benevolently. Cameron fancied there might have been some discreet contact between Ankara and Whitehall. Warning words might have passed the stern lips of Winston Churchill, who would surely have put two and two together and realized that the *Wharfedale*'s presence in Turkey must mean that his wishes were being carried out – always assuming Razakis and Kopoulos hadn't, in fact, taken the great man's name in vain, which Cameron wouldn't put beyond either of them. Yet there had been a shining honesty ... Winston Churchill was unorthodox when he wanted to be, and never mind the Generals and the Admirals. The truth would in all probability never be known, unless in the fullness of time the Captain found himself with a DSC accompanied by some non-committal citation.

Two days later the *Wharfedale* passed through the breakwater into the Grand Harbour. Malta looked the same as ever, if a little more battle-scarred from the Nazi bombs. Sand-coloured around deep blue water and beneath clear skies, Malta was home. They would need to spend some little time in port, refitting in the dockyard after the bomb damage, and replacements would be needed for the dead, now left behind them in the Aegean, and for those who had been wounded and would be transferred to Bighi hospital. That night Cameron went ashore with Bradley. The whole ship's company had been warned by the Captain to keep their mouths sealed against careless talk concerning recent events, and most of them, in the unlikely event of their remaining sober, would heed that warning. In any case, as Bradley said, if they did talk, no one would ever believe them.